Merle Collins is Grenadian. Her published work includes two volumes of poetry, *Because the Dawn Breaks* (1985) and *Rotten Pomerack* (Virago 1992), a novel, *Angel* (1987), *Watchers and Seekers: Creative Writing by Black Women in Britain* (ed with Rhonda Cobham, 1987), and a volume of short stories, *Rain Darling* (1990). She taught at the University of North London until December 1994. She is currently living in the USA and teaches in the Departments of English and Comparative Literature at the University of Maryland.

The COLOUR of FORGETTING

Merle Collins

Published by VIRAGO PRESS Limited July 1995
20 Vauxhall Bridge Road, London SW1V 2SA

A CIP catalogue record for this title is available from the British Library

Typeset by Keystroke, Jacaranda Lodge, Wolverhampton
Printed in Great Britain by Cox & Wyman Ltd, Reading, Berkshire

For my nephew Kevin

BLOOD IN THE NORTH

'Blood in the north, blood to come in the south, and the blue crying red in between.' The woman, dressed in red, stood in the middle of the cemetery, faced north and moaned after delivering her message, turned west and groaned, turned south and shouted, 'The blue crying red in between!' Turned east and cried, 'Lord, have is mercy.'

The child standing at the top of the hill ignored her. He picked up a pebble, rubbed it thoughtfully on the khaki pants of his school uniform, threw it far away over the bushes, down towards the sea.

Carib walked out of the cemetery and past the primary school on her right, down on to the grass and left again below the cemetery to the wall overlooking the steep drop and the sea below. 'Blood in the north,' she shouted, 'and the blue crying red in between.' The goat chewing the grass in the pasture lifted its head and bleated. Kept chewing. Bleated again. Went back to nuzzling the grass.

Carib walked back towards the cemetery, talking conversationally. 'Look at them. Running and jumping. Jumping and screaming. You hear the voices coming up from the bush? Forgotten and consoled. Forgotten and drownded. And the blue crying red in between.'

She stood there in her red dress and red headtie, looking up at the blue sky and down towards the blue of the sea.

The informed observer – and most observers had some basic information by the time they came to visit Leapers' Hill – would guess that she was talking about the Caribs. The Amerindian people, who, long ago, had escaped their French pursuers by jumping off the cliff into the sea. Since then, legend had it, the sea in that part of the island was particularly angry sometimes, churned up with remembering. At times, on the calmest of days, there would be a shout when some not particularly enterprising swimmer went just a little beyond the shallows, and disappeared. Often it would be ·days before the body was recovered.

People trekked often to this spot on the hill when they visited the island of Paz. They were greeted with overgrown splendour, the green so lustrous that it was impossible to see exactly where the drop began, and what, precisely, was happening below. Generally, in response to the question about where the Caribs had jumped, people answered, around here so, indicating the expanse of green splendour.

Carib's shout of 'forgotten and drownded' was in the circumstances perfectly understandable. A people who had given the island such a proud memory had on the spot no monument to their bravery but the voice of the woman called Carib, who may or may not have been a descendant by blood. She, and her mother before her, and, it was rumoured, her mother before her, had been given the name of Carib because of the regular pilgrimage to this hill, named Leapers' Hill in memory of the brave Amerindians. The Caribs were thus not quite forgotten, having as their shrine an entire hill, verdant with undergrowth.

4

Less understandable was Carib's comment about 'forgotten and consoled'. But she may have been thinking of her own lonesome shout to her spirit friends as a consolation of sorts. Or it may even have been a forlorn plea for the needed consolation. There was little enough of that. People had grown up with Carib's voice and its endless effort to kick-start their memory. She had become as much a backdrop to their daily trials as was the bush throttling Leapers' Hill, or the buses racing along the main street of the little town of Mon Repos, or the laughter of the fishermen in the bay, or the shout of women being drastic with children who just wouldn't hear, or the voices of the little ones in the schoolroom just near to Leapers' Hill, practising the words to the song 'Hail Paz, Our Land, Our Joy'.

'Blood in the north, blood to come in the south, and the blue crying red in between.'

In the face of this gloomy prophecy, the person coming upon her standing there in the cemetery says, 'Eh-eh, Carib, you there still? I say you gone down town today, you know.'

Because Carib took her message to town too, often. Town was Paz City, the island's capital. Her main spot there for preaching was the market square, near to the monument built to honour those who had died in the wars. Carib would stand there, surrounded by shouts for 'two bunch ah sive and thyme, please,' 'a pound of dry peas, me dear,' questions about 'how that pile ah sorrel small so', exhortations to 'dress up a little lemme reach the coconut' or, 'move you backside lemme get in the bus, nuh'. Unmoved by all this activity, Carib would survey the scene from the top of a box placed near to the war memorial.

Turning right around so that all of the market could hear,

she would shout her message: 'Honour our children. Honour them when the war that they fight in is war for a place they call the world, and honour them when is war for us here self, that not even in the world. Woe is me! Blood in the north, you know. And look at the blue. Crying red in between.'

In Paz City as in Mon Repos, as in Soleil, the second town, or any other place that Carib preached, people asked when they remembered, 'What is this word she have there that she always saying, about blue crying red in between?' Nobody knew for sure, since Carib wasn't a person you asked to explain things. Well, you could ask. There's no law against that, but you wouldn't be answered. Carib gave information at random, when the spirit moved her, and not when someone else thought it might be required. In this way, she avoided the usual pitfall, avoided, that is, talking nonsense, and said only what was often unintelligible, but was spoken with such intensity that it clearly made a great deal of sense to her. 'Blood in the north, blood in the south, and the blue crying red in between.'

Realising it was pointless to question, people resorted to reasoning, and came to the conclusion, especially when Carib dressed in red and stood on a hill – on heights, for example, like the locations of the old forts, which were strategically placed around Paz City and its harbour – that one blue had to be the blue that she looked up to, the sky, and the other the one that she looked down on, the sea. And she, Carib, the red tears wept from the blue above, poised to drop into the blue below. And then they came back to the north and south idea and said, Well, the north is the place called Carib's Leap. The south? Carib mad no ass, you know. It don't make no sense trying to figure out what she saying.

6

Carib liked to preach at the locations of monuments. There were other places, in Paz City especially, that called her attention. One favourite spot was West India House, built to honour one of the country's leaders associated with the idea of a Caribbean federation. 'Blood to come in the south,' Carib announced from the steps of West India House, 'and the whole West Indies in tears! Look at that! Lord have is mercy! All the sea out there crying red in between. Red. Red. Red. Lord have is mercy! Lord! Have mercy!'

And the young people passing by on the street, unable to resist the pull of this rhythmic invitation, shouted back, bring down percy! Bring down! Percy!

Some days Carib walked through Unity Tunnel, built since the end of the nineteenth century to join the two halves of Paz City. She walked down the centre of the tunnel, stopping the traffic that was always streaming through. Lifting her hands up in the darkness, she cried, 'Let there be light! And light there was none. Unity is strength! But strength there is none. And you know, all-you, oh, the blue crying red in between.'

Once, an irate driver came out of his vehicle with a length of iron in his hand, raising it high above his head directly behind Carib. But those who were trying to squeeze through the dark tunnel, on either side of the traffic, ignored both him and Carib, concerned only to get by. Other drivers sat in their cars leaning on the horns, not even bothering to go out to try and restrain him. They knew, you see, that was just a big voose he making, and that he, like them, would wait until Carib got whatever it was out of her system and moved on. Sometimes, especially if this happened on a Saturday, when traffic was really busy, the police, alerted, would come and lead her gently away, saying, 'OK, Carib, OK,' while Carib

7

warned: 'Blood coming in the south, I tell you, you know, and the blue crying red in between.' And the policeman would hold her arm more firmly and say, 'All right, Carib. All right. Cool.'

It was mostly little children and old people who took Carib seriously. To children, Carib was like one of those strange creatures introduced to them because they live in the imagination of grownups. Lajabless, the woman with one good foot and one cow foot who carried away men whose eyes were too big in their head, or loupgarou, who sucked your blood in the night, or Santa Claus, who appeared only at Christmas time from a land far away, who came to children but made himself visible only to grownups. Carib, with her long dress, usually red, white or blue, although sometimes she wore green or gold, constantly muttering to herself, or stopping in the middle of the road to turn right around and shout strange words to the four corners, seemed to them to inhabit the same kind of space as these other creatures. But she was one they could see, and they clung to their mothers' hands or skirts when she was about. The more fearful rushed under the bed for safety.

In the dreams of one little boy, known as Thunder to the people of Content, a village not far from Mon Repos, red words came out of Carib's mouth and curled around her head, shooting up into the sky. And sometimes in Thunder's dream Carib's head grew, bigger and bigger, longer and longer. Her toenails became sharp and curved and gripped the gravestones at Leapers' Hill, where Thunder had seen her and heard her preach. He would wake screaming, 'Thunder! Thunder, Mama, thunder.' Carib had assumed the proportions of the thing most fearful to him, and to him, thunder was by far the hugest and noisiest of fearful things. But time will come. Time will pass. And tongue will tell the story of thunder.

For most children, the kind of fear Thunder had of Carib lasted only while they were very small. By the time they were six or seven years old, they had generally grown into their parents' attitudes, and accepted the inexplicable with equanimity.

The people who were really old and had little interest left in the things of the world didn't usually hear Carib in the market square and other public places, but they would lift their heads and listen from inside their houses when they heard her passing along the street. They would push aside the window curtains a little and ask, 'Who dat, nuh? Is Carib? What she saying there?' And some young person around would give a long steupes and answer, 'Who know? Talking stupidness as usual.' And the older ones said, 'She great-grandmother had a gift, you know, and even she grandmother too. Is not steupes at all. All-you young people know everything. Was a real, real gift. Long ago, in the days when it had a lot of land confusion and everybody was trying to claim their piece, was Carib great-grandmother they say that used to act as a warning when things get too hot. Don't watch Carib simple at all.' But the young people said, 'Carib mad, I tell you.'

Willive, Thunder's mother, said in her son's hearing, 'Simple as you see Carib looking there, don't fraid for her at all. I always remember my great-grandaunt, Mamag, God rest her soul, she used to say Carib have a true, true gift. Was she great-grandmother had it before her. Mamag say one time, long, long ago when that Great House on the hill there was jefe Great House, the Madam of the time accuse one of the servants of taking a ring and she fire her. Carib great-grandmother walk

9

right up to the Great House one day and say to the servants in the Boss and Madam presence that the ring right on top of the big clothes press in the master bedroom where the Madam hide it to accuse the girl. And you know is there they find the ring? Everybody amaze. And that was after they make simidimi with glass of water and string and other thing that they say prove is the girl that take the ring. So the knowledge Carib have is not joke knowledge.'

'You see thing? People say the grandmother and the mother had the gift little bit, too, but is like the mother couldn't control it, so she go and get kind of bazoodee like, you know. They say sometimes the gift skip a generation or two, but Mamag used to say that we must listen to Carib. And I believe her. Is a gift Carib have. You see this son I have there? Thunder? Is Carib and Mamag that explain to me about the thunder that he so fraid of, and our family is one example of how the prophecy does fulfil. I not saying we family did rich or anything, but it did starting to look up, you know. And look now, nobody in the family prospering. Was land confusion, you see. Confusion right inside the family. And was the same Carib, the great-grandmother self, that walk through the night them times, shouting out, Blood in the land! And warning people to be careful. A nation divided against itself, she used to preach in those times, shall not stand. But what you think people say in those days? She mad no ass. You think they listen? Nuh! She mad no ass. Is a story that come down to me. Is a story I know. Carib? Carib not mad.'

The story that came down to Willive through the generations and made her believe that Carib did in fact have this gift of prophecy that people seemed to accept mainly when it happened in the Bible, was the story of the village and in particular the story of a family named Malheureuse. It was Willive's family story, although now the Malheureuse family name was not there much and Willive, for example, though Malheureuse blood, was a Mrs Janvier, and her son Thunder was really William Janvier. But even if the name gone, the story remain and the spirit remain.

Thunder's earliest memory was of running to hold his mother when it rained. Of hiding his face in her skirt to keep out the sound of thunder. 'Thunder, Mammy, thunder,' he cried. Sometimes there was no thunder, but to him rain and clouds gathering behind the mountain suggested thunder, and he would grip Willive's skirts with both hands and, head burrowing into her, refuse to be dislodged.

When Thunder was about six years old, while the great-grandaunt Mamag was still alive, Willive took him to see Carib. She was becoming increasingly worried about her son, was beginning to think that it wasn't just a child's understandable fear of a sudden, inexplicable noise and was considering taking him to the Shango people, to see if they could do anything for him, perhaps remove from him whatever spirit it was that might be haunting him. Or even asking the priest to pray for him, and leave a lighted candle on the altar. It was Mamag who said, 'I believe I have a idea what do the boy. Bring him and see Carib. People think she mad but I believe she know what she saying. Is not just to move the spirit if is spirit that on him, is to know what it want. Bring him and see Carib.'

Carib had a little house in between the cocoa trees, just below the Anglican church. It was church land, but the church took no rent and left Carib alone. Her great-grandmother, legend had it, had appeared there one day coming out of the hills surrounding Content. She was about three months'

11

pregnant then. It was the time when that land there still had sugar cane, but was beginning to be planted up with cocoa. The authorities of the Anglican church, which controlled the land, had looked on as this woman gathered bits of board from wherever she could and put together a precarious triangular-like structure in the cocoa, just below the church. When the deacon realised she was sleeping inside of it, he asked a few of the youth in the village to lend a hand, and, as uncommunicative as she had been, they appeared one day and helped her to straighten the structure, put up strong wood as pillars to give it some kind of foundation, changed its shape from triangle to square and left the woman to finish it off. The woman had remained silent when the deacon tried to engage her in conversation during the construction work but after the end of the week, when he opened the rectory door that Sunday morning, he found on the step a plant in an old milk-pan, tied around with a red ribbon. The plant was the shame bush, the prickly bush which was open as long as you didn't touch it. If you did, it closed in on itself and slept for a while, until it judged that the danger was past, when it opened up again. The deacon held the plant in his hand and looked down the hill towards the woman's house, then turned and put it on a shelf inside.

Since then, the generations had lived there, but it seemed now that the line was finished, because Carib was fifty-ish and she had no children. When you see that, said Mamag, the work they come to do finish.

When Mamag and Willive went to Carib's house, she met them outside, in the clearing under the trees. Mamag said, 'Is the boy, Carib. Thunder in his head. He fraid thunder. Bad bad. What you think it is?'

12

Carib looked long at Thunder, where he stood with his back to her and his arms as far as they could go around his mother. She said to Mamag, 'I know all-you was coming today, you know. I see you in sleep. To tell you the truth, what they telling me about him is not a lot more than what you know already. But I will tell you.' Carib sat down on a big stone in the yard, closed her eyes. 'Sit down,' she said.

Mamag sat on a tree-stump near to Carib. Willive tried to move, but Thunder wouldn't let her. She was trying to pull his arms away when Mamag motioned her to leave him and stay there.

Carib started to moan. Long and low. A sort of groan that started somewhere inside her belly and came up to her throat. Thunder held on to his mother with both hands, burying his face in her skirt. Willive put her hand on his head and stayed silent.

Carib opened her eyes and said, 'Blood in the north, and the blue crying red in between.'

Frightened for her son, Willive found herself wanting to say, 'Well, we know that already.'

Carib looked at the back of the little head hidden in his mother's skirt and said quietly, 'Sometimes the children who should know most is the ones that know the least. Walk back. Walk back over all of the story with him. Is the younger ones to stop the blue from crying red in between, but them self looking outside. They not listening inside here self. Is not that he don't know, but his head will get twist with all kind of other things he reading. He go be all right in the end, though. Red all around him, oh God, red all around him, you know. But is he, and others like him, will stop the blue from crying red in between. He go look like he don't know. But he go be all

13

right. Walk back with him. Walk back.' Carib stood up and turned around in the yard, her hands to her head. 'Lord! What does do these children? What does do us who should know? Thunder. Thunder in the night. Thunder in his head. Night of thunder and rain. Oh, God, blood on his face. Blood! Blood! Blood in the north!'

Her shout was echoed in the cocoa as Thunder started bawling. Willive lifted him up, saying to Mamag, 'I think I better go now.' Mamag looked at Carib.

'The story there,' Carib said. 'The story will come out, anyway. Is he and the younger ones, you know, to keep the blue from crying red in between. Walk back. Walk back and tell him the story.'

And Mamag said to Willive, 'You could go. Go. Go home with him. We will talk later.'

The story that Mamag heard that night was a lot of what she knew already, because was the Malheureuse story. She and Willive had already talked about a lot of it. Thunder, Carib said, would have to know it all, over the years. The thunder he was hearing was the thunder inside him. Wasn't his alone, but the spirits letting him hear it and it would only stop when he found a way of understanding the spirits that lived inside him. 'You could only help,' said Carib, 'by telling him everything you know. But is all right. Is a reason why they making him hear the thunder. Mightn't even be in your time, Mamag, but you will know. He going be all right. Walk back with him over the Malheureuse story. Is he and others like him, here and to come, to stop the blue from crying red in between.'

THE MALHEUREUSE STORY

Mixture in the blood of the story. Not simple. Where we starting is after the beginning. Man come so they didn't call him man. Call him slave. Slave get name. John Bull.

John Bull was a slave that get killed in the market square in Paz City since the days when the Spanish catholics used to listen to the rage in the place and call it Pax, like a joke. *Pax tecum.* Peace be with you. Pax. With a slap. Take that.

And one day peace exploded in the head of a white carpenter man scratching to make a living in the heat in Pax. A man named Malheureuse. And he looked around. For something that was nothing just to shake and to cuff and to bring peace back to his head. Malheureuse found something. John Bull. Beat John Bull in his head with a stick. Beat the slave in his head until the brain cave in, the soul disappear into waiting and body lie down there in the dust with the face cover up with the red of the blood.

Afterwards, the story go that while John Bull getting licks Papa God blue sky open all of a sudden and the rain come down. But where he lie down there in the dust with the red on his face is like the rain make the red more thick instead of washing it away. Like the blue was crying red. But some people again say that is nonsense. The red stay in truth, but is really that somebody lift up John Bull and put him to lie down under the awning of a house on the sidewalk. But the thing is, the red remain, didn't get wash away by the rain. But anyway, peace come back to Malheureuse head. Because when doctor examine and court had its say, it turn out that wasn't beat that kill John Bull. Was suffocate he suffocate. Suffocation kill him. And drunkenness. Too much fluid in the mouth and the wind-pipe suffocate that slave. Nothing to say. Peace come back to Malheureuse.

And time come and pass. One and one become two become four become eight. Every different thing start to look like same thing. Time come and pass. Time bring a boss-man Malheureuse to a Great House. The Malheureuse blood pass on to the slave women generation that Boss-man Malheureuse breed. To John Bull nation. Mixture in the blood of the story. After a while people walking in the cane and can't tell the difference between some of Malheureuse generation and John Bull nation. And peace on every face even if brain boxing and breaking, *pax*. Pax become Paz. Become city. Become Paz City.

And in the mountain, Crapaud down in the mud of the drain only keep saying: 'Wait a while', while Monkey, up on the tree, keep saying: 'No, things cool'. Things cool for Monkey, you see, because the breeze always in Monkey face. So Monkey not wrong, and Crapaud not wrong. Is not a question of right and wrong, really. Crapaud just in a different position. Close to the ground, it right on top of the heat. And whatever happening, it always hearing the pounding. So while Monkey saying things cool, Crapaud always croaking hold on, hold on, something coming.

Monkey say cool breeze
Crapaud say wait a while

Monkey say cool breeze . . .

But truth to tell, the mountain is really cool. Even Crapaud
feeling the damp. But the other thing is, it hearing the heat.
From way back, the Scots adventurers, coming long after the
paths had been cleared of Amerindian footprints, thought they
could feel something sinister in this place. The rest of the
island hot, hot, but the mountain cool, cool. And the hillsides
up there didn't like the sugar-cane. And the African people not
afraid of the brambles and the frog croaks and the monkeys
swinging far above and all the strange animal sounds.

The adventurers had tried to change the magic by a re-
naming. Or a naming, you might call it, since by the time they
came, the Caribs were gone, the French had left, and the Scots
knew no other name. Arthur's Seat, they called it, like some
place they knew at home, and it became theirs. But not for
long, and never, really. When the African people whom they
called slaves disappeared from the estate, the mountain hugged
and hid them even in spite of the magic of the naming. Or
perhaps the Africans just knew better how to talk with the
spirits of this land that people said the Caribs, who had another
name too, used to call Camerhogne. You hear it? Camerhogne.
Like a howl. Like music. Camerhogne. Who know what is
what? And how to know if you can't hear voices in the wind?
If a howl could frighten you to cowering and music is not really
something that you listening for?

And then when time come and pass and who in charge
decide to sell off the land that not so good, well, things

change. By this time so, wasn't Arthur's Seat people calling it, since the name meant nothing to them, but Attaseat, claiming the magic. And because not too many of the big people really wanted mountain land, lots in Attaseat were bigger than the one or two acres available elsewhere.

The man they called Jim-Bull Malheureuse acquired fifteen acres. Jim-Bull Malheureuse. Big man. Walking almost as tall as he had seen Boss-man Malheureuse walk on the plantation. And why not? His fair-skin self, and the people that know, say is not just the white Malheureuse name he have, the Malheureuse blood in him for true. That self-same Malheureuse they saying that descend from people that do dangerous things in the early days. Ordinary, but dangerous. Malheureuse blood. Not jefe blood in the beginning. Ordinary white carpenter Malheureuse to start with. Long, long ago. But tongue say is not long time that matter, is later.

And if Boss-Man Malheureuse could walk tall with the story of his ancestor in his soul, who say Jim-Bull, that get the blood not from the asking, don't have the right? And when time come again and pass again, is Jim-Bull Malheureuse that hold his head high and vowing that this nigger Malheureuse go be somebody in this country. And so, Jim-Bull, Malheureuse however he become that, and Malheureuse because is the only name he know, stretch up on tiptoe and he hang he hat.

One child they have, Jim-Bull and his wife, and, to tell you the truth, they didn't want more. This, after all the hard times and the landless generations, was the time to hold on to your land and work it for another generation. One was enough. Not that they do anything to make it stay so. Is just that God self see is so it should be. And from the time he born their little boy looking like he was here before. Look at that face, people saying. That not no little child all-you have there, nuh. Is a old, old man.

Two years old when the land came to his father Jim-Bull Malheureuse in 1844, Oldman had never known the worst of times, and his father always told him that the family had a name to keep up. An inheritance to cherish. Wasn't easy to acquire. So is to cherish.

The hillsides liked the yam and the dasheen and tannia. And don't talk about the oranges. They could make your mouth water with the way they looking like the rain bless them and the sun is their father. And if children go all up there in the mountain to pelt at the tree, is just that they couldn't help it.

And time coming still and passing still. In the branches, Monkey, head up in the air, chattering, cool breeze. Crapaud no longer listening for dogs and horses and footsteps hunting men who had run from plantations, but keeping its head to the ground none the less, and whispering in that croaky voice, 'Wait a while, I tell you! Wait a while!'

More time come and pass. Oldman Malheureuse was a fine, upstanding man in the district. A married man with his five children. Mayum was the middle one. So there were two on either side of Mayum. Caiphas was the first. The second was Isidora. After Mayum there was Adolphus, who became Son-Son, and then Magdalene, the youngest, who later became Mamag because people used to call her Ma Magdalene. From the time she little. Ma Magdalene. Because she used to listen to what big people talking with a face that say she know more than she should know. In the beginning, the father used to shout at her to keep out of big people business, but the mother Magdalene say quiet-like, Leave her, she was here before. And

Oldman hear that often enough to understand. So he leave Mamag alone, let her continue what she begin from long time.

From her childhood days, Mamag used to run down the hill near to the road and listen when the woman who lived in the cocoa under the Anglican church walking up and down along the road shouting. The woman everybody called Carib. To Mamag, living up there in the bush, this woman Carib was like another country. A new country. Always saying something strange and new and mixed-up and exciting-sounding and frightening. Land confusion, Carib used to say, is not easy confusion, you know, and in this country here, land is like life and the way we inherit this piece, that piece, look at it, the blue crying red in between. The two side not together even when they inside each other. One fighting the other. Lord have is mercy! The blue crying red in between.

In those long-ago days, little Mamag used to put down the bucket or the yew or the pail or the broom or whatever she have in she hand and rush all the way down the hill to the road when she hear Carib voice. Sometimes Carib used to have her little girl walking with her. One time Carib talk about a place called Leapers' Hill, where long ago some Carib people jump off a cliff rather than give themself up. Carib say how spirits always there moaning and weeping. And how people don't even hear them. And as the mother talking, the little Carib cover her face and she moaning. And Mamag watching and listening with her mouth open. And she watching, too, how some of the young men by the rum shop up the hill lean against the door and shout out. 'We hearing them, Carib. We hearing the spirits, *wi*. They sounding just like you.' Was like that. People didn't take Carib seriously, really. Not until after. Long after when time come and pass, after little people like Mamag and the little Carib who was older than Mamag become big people and Carib get old. After Carib the mother dead. Long after. When people remember.

Talk pass around that the last thing the old woman Carib say as she lie down dying in the little house under the Anglican church was, 'Blood coming, yes. Blood coming in our time. Blood come before, but is we that bringing blood this time. With help from outside, perhaps. But is we. Who gone coming back and dividing. And the blue crying red in between.'

For a while after Carib the mother died, the daughter used to walk up the road and sprinkle holy water that people say she take from the font in the Mon Repos Catholic church. And she would say in a voice that sound like her mother, 'Take a blessing, Attaseat. Take a blessing. The blue crying red in between. The blue crying red in between.'

But people took Carib the daughter even less seriously than they had taken her mother. Is a mad family, they saying, and this one keeping up the tradition. But still Carib muttered to people she met in the street, 'Watch out, you know. The blue crying red in between.' And Mamag notice that while Carib the mother had preached around the Mon Repos and Content area, the daughter started walking all over the island, spending days and even months away. Sometimes for days Mamag didn't hear her voice in the road. The years pass like that. The Mon Repos people getting less and less impressed, especially when Carib reappeared pregnant after one of these trips away.

Now, when she stood in the crossroads by the Nutmeg Station warning about the blue crying red in between, the young men on the bridge shouted, 'In between you leg it crying, Carib?' And they laughed and pulled on their crotches, hearing less and less of the prophecy. 'Who Carib think she fooling?' they wondered. 'Everybody know that prophecy and pregnancy don't mix. Prophecy? Who breed her? The angel Gabriel?' Gabriel must be cover his face and either blush or look shame, depending, when the men shouting to Carib by the crossroads. Undaunted, Carib kept warning about the blood to come in the north. A nation divided against itself, she said, cannot stand.

And while Mamag there watching what the years doing with the Carib generation, a lot of thing happening, too, in her own generation with the Malheureuse name. Oldman wife Magdalene, Mamag mother, come and die first, but by that time all the children drink water already. Mamag, the last one, big enough woman already. So it was no big hardship for them. They could take care of themselves.

But what make thing come and turn ole mass was the will Mr Oldman leave behind when he die. *Amway bonjay!*

The children cut up the land as they suppose to, piece for this one, piece for that one, another piece for the other one, and so on. The eldest one, Caiphas, organise it. And Caiphas never bring any confusion in the family. Everybody know the Malheureuse family to be a fine upstanding one in the area.

Well, time come and pass. The Malheureuse family not so well-off as before, because the land that used to belong to one man in house with wife and children now divide up between a lot of different people, so each one had less, but still, they not badly off. Better than most. And then it come about that Caiphas, Mamag brother, the oldest Malheureuse son, come and dead. Anyway, the different parts of the family still living good. Not rich, you know, but living, and eating. And that good. The land that belong to Caiphas go to who he say is his heirs and everything was in order. The first son of Caiphas, in fact, his only son, only child, come and travel. He leave to work in island overseas, in Cuba, they say. And then, lo and behold, one day sometime in about 1930, this son return. And is then confusion begin.

This boy of Caiphas own start to push trouble. He dig up Mr Oldman will, and say that the land is wrongly divided. Some should get more, some should get less, and some should have nothing at all.

According to the will, you know, as the son read and interpret it careful careful, only lawful children and their descendants should inherit of this land. The unlawful had no place. No rights.

And was when this talk spread abroad that people start to say, But this is something here, yes. He gone so long where he gone, now he coming back an dividing! And is then they remember. What mother tell them, what auntie remember, what cousin say, what grandmother and grandfather declare Carib did prophecy when she dying. Land confusion. Coming back and dividing. Lord! She must be see it in dream?

But by this time, when people turn around, there was no prophecy to listen to. Carib the daughter had disappeared one day somewhere on the eastern side of the island. She drown, people say, when she went to feed the lake. No one know if she walk in and the lake take her, or if she fall in. The story goes that she disappear in the lake.

Her daughter, who had taken to walking, like the mother and grandmother before her, all around Paz, still lived in the cocoa down below the church. But although she was walking and talking, this talking was for the most part a muttering, to herself, as if the prophecy turned in on itself, eating itself up inside, not knowing how to get out.

Mamag, the youngest one of the Malheureuse family, say is the prophecy that send her dotish. And remembering the mother and grandmother, Mamag used to groan when talk go around about how the men of Content dragging the younger Carib off into the bush whenever they feel like it. And afterwards they laughing about how, whole way through while they wining on top, Carib below muttering about the blue crying red in between.

But it was when Carib get pregnant that Mamag decide enough is enough. She went one day and took Carib away to the mental asylum in Paz City, saying, Poor thing, at this stage, she will better off there. And every two weeks or so, Mamag used to go down to Paz City with something for Carib and, later on, for the little girl that the authorities decide to move to the children's ward in the hospital, since they didn't know what else to do with her. Mamag, by this time, had her own family confusion, and her five children, to deal with. Five children, yes. One story not stopping to wait while another one crossing it.

But let us see how the story of the Malheureuse family confusion go. Of the generation, Caiphas own was lawful. Isidora had one child, and she was not lawful. Mayum had two, Ti-Moun and Cosmos, with his lawful wife, but both of them born before they married. Those that Son-Son acknowledge were two lawful ones, inside his house. Mamag had five, and all of them unlawful. But who the matter really rest with, who the story really turn upside down, was Mayum children. By this time, Mayum Malheureuse, that is the middle child, the second son, was dead. But his children, Ti-Moun and Cosmos, inherit their father land. Not much, an acre and a half. But enough. Enough. *Amway bonjay!* Thing turn ole mass.

And who the wind keep howling about now is Mayum two, Ti-Moun and Cosmos. If people listen, they will hear the wind telling the story that cause so much confusion. Trouble inside is not new story. Is story that there from time. Nation shall rise against itself.

TI-MOUN AND COSMOS

'Look at that, eh!' people used to say. 'Same mother, same father, but they different as chalk and cheese. From the time they were small.' But in spite of that, or perhaps because of that, they got on well together. It was as if they knew from early that they weren't struggling for the same sunlight. Living like they did in the heart of the mountain, they had seen trees grow together enough to understand.

Plant a breadfruit tree by itself and it would grow to normal height. Plant it near to a bois canot and you would see the two of them stretching up and up, each one struggling to catch more of the sunlight.

Is the same way immortelle and cocoa behave. Plant the mortelle in the middle of the cocoa to give it shade, and even though the cocoa knows it needs the shade and can't battle with the mortelle, it would keep shooting upwards, until the mortelle, sure of its destiny, breaks free and goes higher, and higher. And when two trees battle it out together, once one gets on top, it spreads its branches, showing its colours and taking strength from the sunshine. And the other one struggling, kind of pitiful like, to thrive in its shadow. Although cocoa never really look pitiful, you know. Just accepting. Knowing that shadow is its life. Is just what it need to survive.

It know, you know. But is the way of things. It still not giving up too easy on the fight for sunlight. After all, a fight is a fight.

Cosmos and Ti-Moun were planted apart. Not wanting each other's sunlight, they grew apart, each wondering at the other's branching. Cosmos watched the way people would come right up to the house to call and ask Ti-Moun if he would go down to their garden to pick a breadfruit for them, to pick two baskets of oranges, to come and help them crack cocoa.

'*Gentle*man!' he teased his brother, with a drawling emphasis on the gentle. 'Gentleman! You expecting you reward in heaven! Me, I know heaven is right here, so I making sure I get mine now. Gentleman!'

Ti-Moun would only smile. Most times, anyway, it was Mamag who came to ask, and he liked his aunt. Not that Cosmos didn't like her too, but as far as Cosmos was concerned, so what? Like is like and work is work.

With five children of her own, Mamag worked hard in the land, but there were some things she needed help with. She wasn't getting younger, and three of her five girls were in town learning to sew. Another one was in Trinidad looking for work and the last one was ready to escape, too. They saw their future in town, in sewing, working behind a shop counter, or going away to some other place.

'Where those girls' father?' Cosmos asked in that laughing way he had. He wouldn't say this to anyone else, but he knew he could say almost anything to his brother and it wouldn't go any further to cause confusion.

'Same place your little girl father is,' Ti-Moun answered him. 'You remember what she look like?'

And Cosmos would laugh, coughing and slapping at his

water-boots. 'Gentleman!' he countered. 'Real gentleman! You know how man is already.'

'Yes,' Ti-Moun would agree. 'I know. That's why I helping Mamag.'

'Better you than me, Mr Ti-Moun. Better you than me.'

'Right,' his brother agreed. 'That is why is me and not you.'

And is so it happen through the years. Cosmos kept laughing. Ti-Moun kept smiling at his brother's laughter. There was no quarrel over land when their father followed their mother to the grave. Ti-Moun enjoyed responsibility. Cosmos didn't. They didn't even worry about dividing the land. Live like brother and brother on the one piece. Some people say that this wasn't a good thing, that you suppose to share and share, know who have what and everybody have their boundary, but the sharing never cause any confusion between them. The two of them live like Jack Sprat and he wife. Is a family like that, though, people said, very loving. Is just so these two boys' father, Mayum and his brother, Son-Son, used to live together. Is a family like that. The youngest one Mamag, always kind of had own way, but still, very much with the family. Is a family like that. Ti-Moun helped Cosmos to build a house, or, to say the thing as it is, built Cosmos a house on the land, while he Ti-Moun self worked the land with his wife and lived in the family house.

By and by, one of the women Cosmos said he loved came to live with him. Because, you know, sometimes is like that. You know the way people used to buy ha'penny of this little plum called penapiece and get a whole handful for this ha'penny? Sometimes is like that with people and trouble. They buy whole handful of a trouble that is penny a piece just because they getting it for ha'penny. So this woman, she come and take Cosmos put on she account. And while Cosmos revelling in the rumshops, Ti-Moun find time to help her get things from the land, as he did for Mamag. You see what I telling you? That is the kind of living you had between Ti-Moun and his brother, two people as different as chalk is different from cheese. Sometimes Papa God does well know who he putting together as relative and relative, as friend and friend. Sometimes, but you can't take put on you account to expect that. Because sometimes again, you have to wonder.

'You must talk to your brother,' Cassandra said to her husband Ti-Moun one day. 'You must talk to him, you know. He making Josephine and those children eat the bread that the devil knead.'

And Ti-Moun answer, 'Josephine know what she taking on when she decide to go and live in house with Cosmos. Cosmos is people you having a good time with if you want, and then let them pass go their way. That is not people you deciding to stay in house with.'

'Talk to him,' insisted Cassandra. 'Is your brother.'

'I talk to him. I talk to him already. Cosmos know what I think about how he living. But that is who he is. People who can't be like that and who can't stand it just have to keep away.'

'God don't make people worthless,' Cassandra give as her opinion. 'Cosmos could change. He just don't-care.'

And Ti-Moun say, 'I ain't know who make people how. But is not this morning Cosmos like that. He so from time. He not bad, you know, he just . . .'

But Cassandra don't let him finish. She feel she know how Cosmos is. So she finish the sentence with: 'Worthless.'

'Well,' and Ti-Moun shrugged, 'Cosmos have to work out his own way.'

'If Josephine know what good for her,' Cassandra feel, 'she would take her children and run as far as she could from that good-for-nothing.'

And Ti-Moun smile at that.

'What so funny?' Cassandra want to know.

'Just the idea of Josephine running with a parcel of four children in a basket,' her husband say. 'Just that idea.'

And Cassandra chuckled. Huh! Chuckle, you know. Like laugh. Well, is so thing is already. Sometimes you just have to decide to see the funny side in spite of everything.

And Cassandra could well see the funny side. In the yard where she grow up in her mother house, Cassandra was always hearing from her great-grandmother next door about the funny side. When things get really bad and Cassandra mother fretting, her great-grandmother used to say, 'Hold up you head. You only think you know trouble. Watch how lucky you is. Look up and laugh in people face. We blood not weak. If we generation couldn't see the funny side of life, not one person live to tell the story.'

'My great-great-grandfather,' she used to say, 'was a man name John Bull. And you see Oldman Malheureuse? Well, is his great-great-grandfather they say that beat this John Bull in he head till he dead in the market in Paz City. Think about that. Well, Oldman don't have nothing to do with that, you know. Is not his mother side of the family. Is the one they say is his father side. Those white Malheureuse. Oldman is the outside set. And with the inside set self it had a rich side and a poor side and Oldman grandfather come and inherit from a uncle. But is the selfsame Malheureuse that kill my great-great-grandfather. Let the cocoa juice run down the side of you mouth make it look greasy, drink water in the river full up you belly and laugh in their face.

'Laugh, child,' she used to say. 'Don't let nothing make you cry.' And she used to say to Cassandra, 'Learn to laugh, you hear, chile. Don't even wait to look see if you find a funny side. Make it up. It don't have no funny side to a man lie down with blood on his face on a night when rain falling with a vengeance and thunder making more noise than anybody could stand. I defy any ordinary person to see the funny side.

'But, child, if you don't learn to play dead and even laugh as if you dotish when the world knock you down, laugh just to witness you funeral, is kill they will kill you in truth. So play dead, me child, and learn to live. Child? Pick sense from nonsense. Play dead and learn to live. And God so strange with the way he does work.' And Cassandra could remember her great-grandmother spitting out the tobacco and laughing. 'You don't hear how Oldman grandmother call he father, she son? Jim Bull! That is woman! Even when she come out under Malheureuse she making sure she keep in she mind the man those Malheureuse kill. Eh! Think about that. That is woman! Jim-Bull in you shirt!'

And everybody that Cassandra talk to serious later on in her life, she tell them the story. And if you listening careful, careful, you will hear that kind of story howling in the wind in villages all over Paz. Is why sometimes the wind would find a hole in an old, old tree and stay there whistling and whistling. The question is, who listening?

It strange, yes. But you listening? Because if you listening good what you will realise from this telling, is that who Ti-Moun with his Malheureuse blood come and marry is somebody that come straight down in a line from the John Bull that mouth say Malheureuse the carpenter kill in the market in Paz City. John Bull who lie down dead in the market on a night full of thunder and rain. You listening? In this country here, I tell you, everything is one thing. So you can't surprise that the blue crying red in between.

But the way how things developing now in Cassandra life, was looking like a new thing. Only looking. New for today. Happen yesterday. But new for Cassandra. That morning, Ti-Moun was talking to his wife and pointing at the house with his chin.

'Willive sleep well early last night. She was gone already when I reach home.'

'Well, yesterday she run about so much with Josephine two little ones! And then in the afternoon we walk down by Mamag. So she tired.'

Ti-Moun unlatched the bottom part of the door. Pushed it open, went back outside and stood looking into the early morning light-darkness.

'I must go, yes,' he saying. 'It getting late. You need more wood to cook today? I must send back a bundle or is all right?'

'Well,' Cassandra answer him, 'Joseph bring a big load yesterday and the other little one carry a bundle almost as big for the mother. I think me and Josephine all right until tomorrow, so don't bother yourself.'

'OK.' Ti-Moun satisfy with that. So he say, 'Well, tell Josephine to send Joseph alone today.'

But Cassandra have another thing that worrying her. She want to know, 'You decide what you will do about what the estate offer? You will take the cocoa land?'

But Ti-Moun head not for taking no extra land from the estate to work. 'No,' he say. 'That is too much work. And is all for them when you look at it. I will take more garden land for meself, and Josephine two big ones there would be able to go with me and help out early in the morning before they go to school.'

And watching how Ti-Moun working hard, Cassandra find she couldn't leave the subject of Cosmos alone. 'You must really talk to your brother, you know. Is a burning shame. A master mason like him, people putting up wall regular enough these days, and he won't even try to go by town and look for work. Is Josephine bursting she tail struggling with the children and doing what she could in the land.'

So Ti- Moun agree. 'All right, I will talk to him again. But I have to go now. Perhaps I should have leave the cows for Cosmos boys to tie out this morning. That making me late. This rate I will never make it to the garden before I go to the estate.'

'OK then,' Cassandra say. 'Go on. I will plant out the peas today. And you must try and dig the potato bank when you come home this evening, so I could put out some potato slip.'

'Yes,' Ti-Moun say, and he sounding tired just thinking. 'Yes. All right.'

Cassandra self thinking that is thanks to the little piece of land, thanks to the fact that both of them working out their soul-case on it, that they able to make things work and to look forward to a bit better life for this little Willive they have there. If wasn't for the land, she thinking, who know what could happen?

It is dew-wet under the cocoa trees when Ti-Moun leaves his home that morning. Monkey chattering, chattering. Crapaud croaking just as loudly. Today it's a competition. One voice tumbling over the other and you can't hear nothing clear. Although Crapaud usually warning to 'wait a while' while monkey saying, 'nuh, man, cool breeze,' it is so confused this morning that Monkey seems to be saying 'wait' and Crapaud saying 'breeze'. The orange trees are pushing their heads up, looking like they want to argue with the nutmeg leaves. Too close to the guava, the peas tree is ducking and bending to taste the light. The mortelle stretching far above the cocoa, spreading out itself alone up there and not needing to struggle. And the dew-tears just washing the faces of the leaves of the cocoa tree.

Monkey say cool breeze
Crapaud say . . .

Afterwards, walking back in her mind over the unfolding of the day, Cassandra feel she could remember that she know something was wrong the moment she see Uncle Son-Son through the window with the stranger.

It must have been the way they stand up down by the mango tree looking around and shaking their heads and talking. Uncle Son-Son lifting his hand and measuring the land with his finger, pointing right around. The stranger, arms akimbo on the sides of his grey flannel jacket, turning right around, planting his feet and looking and nodding.

Cassandra frown, her attention moving only for a little bit to Willive. The child was sitting on the step, putting something into her mouth. And Cassandra thinking, 'What do this child at all? Malaria and all kind of thing flying in the wind, I wonder what nonsense she eating there? Then deciding: Is all right. Only a piece of the bread and cheese plant that she break off from a tin on the step.

The men walk towards the house, still talking, pointing. Cassandra move to the door. Flannel, Papa, she thinking. Flannel he wearing, yes. Huh. Things good with this one.

'Willive,' she say, holding the little girl's hand and pulling her away from the plant, 'leave my flowers alone. I see enough trouble to make them grow. Leave them alone.'

The men stop. The stranger don't even take off his hat. Uncle Son-Son lips smiling. He watching Willive and talking to Cassandra.

'*Kuma u ye*, Madam Ti-Moun? I just passing by with Dolphus. You mightn't really know him. He leave here long time go and work in Cuba. Is my first brother Caiphas, God rest his soul, son. This is Madame Ti-Moun, Dolphus. Where Ti-Moun, Cassandra?'

Cassandra looked from one man to the other. The stranger had hardly looked at her. Arms akimbo again, surveying the land with his eyes. Not like family talking with family. But then, Cassandra thinking, I suppose they mean is Ti-Moun that is their family.

'Ti-Moun at work,' she say.

'What time you expect him?' Uncle Son-Son ask.

And Cassandra tell him, 'Not until late. He does pass in the garden down in the pasture first before he reach.'

Uncle Son-Son want to know, 'So he don't come home to eat?'

Cassandra explain, 'Those children usually bring something for him in the garden.'

'Cosmos' children?' he ask her.

And she answer him yes.

And Uncle Son-Son say, 'Well, tell him we pass. We will talk to him later.' That was all. Tell him we pass. We will talk to him later.

Sometimes rain falls like a blessing. But that wasn't the way it fell for the rest of the day. It pushed deep into the mud and tumbled down the hillsides. It pressed the leaves of the cocoa tree towards the ground. It slapped against the galvanise of the roof. It left the bread and cheese plants soaked and beaten.

That day, Willive pulled at everything she could find. She was at that kind of age, just a few months before her second birthday, but it had never seemed such a problem before. Today she pulled down the ycw of water from the washstand, screaming when the jug hit her on the head. She overturned the centre table, knocking the vase of plastic flowers on to the floor. She pulled at the cloth on the shelf and nearly broke the goblet. Cassandra kept rushing from the kitchen, through the rain and over the barrier into the house.

'Willive!' she shouting. 'If you not careful, child, it going to be will-die this day, you know! Pull you backside in the corner, here.'

But Willive only screamed harder, holding on to the barrier with the snot running from her nose, and looking through the rain at Cassandra moving to and fro in the kitchen.

Towards evening, the showers ceased to a steady drizzle. Night, with the small lamp burning on the table in the hall, the big lamp on the shelf inside. Willive was at last half asleep, lying face down on her lap, when Cassandra heard sounds from the yard. A shuffling. Cosmos' dog barking down the hill. She pushed back the chair and struggled to her feet. She put the fretting Willive in her bed on the floor just inside the room door, rushed back to open the outside door.

'Mamag, yes. Mamag!' Cassandra say. 'Mamag? What happen? Something happen?'

Ti-Moun, too, with Mamag. And he just walked past them inside. Not even wiping his feet on the crocus bag in front of the door. Walk past Cassandra and sit down in the armchair in his working clothes.

Cassandra move the small lamp to the centre table. Ti-Moun lift his head and look long at the flame, look, look at the smoke clouding the small chimney. And then he turn around to look at Mamag.

And he ask, 'But they can't do it, Mamag? They can't do it? They can't just cut me out of something I work so hard for?'

'Child,' Mamag say, 'I don't know for sure. They shouldn't be able to, but from the way I know Will and land does work, perhaps they could do it. We going to go in town tomorrow and find out what is what, but I don't want to raise you hopes. Perhaps they could well do it. Son-Son is me brother, and I know how he could be covetous. People does look in from the outside and say how things sweet. But is who inside that know. I know Son-Son always feel that you father was the favourite one and, well, everything not always simple in family. I not going to tell you they can't do it. I don't know. We have to see.'

Cassandra want to say something. She want to ask them why they talking over her head and what they talking about. But she fraid. Ti-Moun sit down there in the armchair now staring at her. And without saying nothing, he say everything. And without hearing nothing, Cassandra hear everything. And she just feel she want to cry. And eventually Ti-Moun just push himself up out of the chair and walk into the room to say good-night to Willive.

And now, Cassandra's eyes walking all over Mamag face. She thinking of the two men who bring the rain. She look out into the night and make the sign of the cross for protection.

Mamag explain: 'Son-Son come by me with Caiphas boy. I hear they come here. The thing is, child, they want to take the land. The Will say is not for bastard to inherit, and Ti-Moun and Cosmos both born before Mayum and their mother married. Who inherit must be solid people who right inside the family and know what they about.'

'But . . . ' and Cassandra kneel down near to Mamag's chair, looking up at the older woman. 'But, Mamag,' she say, 'but, Mamag, ent their father married their mother?'

'Yes,' Mamag agree, 'but they both bastard born.'

'But, Mamag,' Cassandra asking, 'Mamag, people could do thing like that? They could take from you what is rightfully yours like that?'

And Mamag saying, 'I believe they could do it, child. I believe they could do it. Is to hold on and see what will happen, but I know my brother and my sister Isidora. Rightful look as if is something for the law to decide.'

'But Isidora have bastard too!' Cassandra pointing out.

But Mamag explain the thing as she see it good and long. She say, 'Isidora don't care. And from what I hear they feel they have better ideas for the land, and they believe they could find the money to make more out of it. I think what they was trying to do was to divide one against the other, to find a way to leave it with Ti-Moun and then work along with Ti-Moun if he would agree to cut Cosmos out, but you know that wouldn't work. Anyway, I don't know if they could have make that stick with the law. So from what I understand they will try to make them lose everything. Is as if they think is a good they

43

will be doing for the family land, child, and for the family name, if they take the land. Imagine that! They feel they could manage it better. Child, is so this Will and this greedy for land is. Why you think I long ago sell the piece I inherit and buy another piece? Just so that my children sure to have something that nobody could say is family own. I know how land confusion is no respecter of blood. Family does kill family in this business, all for the good of land and for the family name. But I don't want to put bad mouth on this thing. God prevent that from happening.'

And Mamag cross herself and kiss her fingers. 'I wanted to make sure,' she say, 'that my bastard and them have land to inherit, so I get out of it. But I didn't think to say that it could touch Ti-Moun and Cosmos, being as their father married the mother. I just didn't think to talk to Ti-Moun about it. Beg God pardon, but all those Son-Son and them must suffer for what they doing. Who know where they hiding their bastard? Who know how much bastard they have that they satisfy to think is not really children? And they making confusion with other people bastard for land.'

'But . . . ' Cassandra start off as if she want to say something, but she not sure what. There were no words. The trouble had walked up without warning.

'Is all right,' Mamag whisper, 'is all right. Take it easy. Try to make him take it easy. Something bound to work out. Don't lie down give them. The thing is, chile, if two man-crab can't stay in the same barrel, one does usually have to move out to give the other one room. And let's hope is not Ti-Moun and Cosmos that have to get out. But it have one thing I didn't tell you, you know. I don't know if all-you ready to consider that. But Son-Son apparently saying that if Ti-Moun want he could

44

stay in the house on the land here, just that the land won't be his and it would be Son-Son house he staying in as a favour. I know that is confusion, because it mean you could get throw out any time. I don't know what you-all will decide. But is all right. Take courage, child. Even self is so it have to happen, take courage. Something bound to work out.'

Cassandra didn't doubt that. What she was afraid of was what that something would be.

LAW IS LAW

Law is law. Son-Son, one of the lawful heirs to the Malheureuse property, says that the law should be respected. And his sister Mamag must, he thinks, also be taught some respect. Right inside of a rumshop she challenged him one day. Bad how it is, she is still his sister, so when he hear her opening her mouth laughing *kya kya* in rumshop joke the evening, he had to tell her something.

'Go home,' Magda, he said. 'Go and see after your children, nuh.'

'Beg pardon?' Mamag looked as if she couldn't believe she was hearing right. Then she put her right arm akimbo on her hip, throw back her head and laugh *kya kya kya* worse than before. 'But wait! You talking to me, Mr Shabin? You really talking to me? Tell me something, nuh. My children ever ask you for cold water? Because if they ask you, tell me right now and I will sort them out meself. They ever ask you for a shilling to drink tea?'

And Son-Son wanted to know, 'Who you calling Shabin?'

So Mamag explained. 'But it don't have nobody else in here with that shabin colour. Who else I could be calling Shabin? You forget that was your nickname growing up?'

A couple of the men chuckled softly. Some moved their

bodies just a little bit on the bench. One man said to the shop-keeper, 'Give me a eighth, there, boy.' And he was sounding like he not in the shop at all and not hearing what going on.

And some people obviously enjoying the ole talk but trying to look as if they somewhere else. But some right in the middle. One of the women was saying, 'But I didn't know that. I didn't know that was you nickname. But anyway, what do? Is to be expected people will call you Shabin, Son-Son. It don't have nothing in that.'

Son-Son ask his sister, 'Why you don't go home and mind you little bastard and them, eh, Magda?'

And Mamag already. In those days as later, she had a plaster for every sore. 'You that so fraid bastard blood,' she ask her brother, 'how you managing walking around every day with Malheureuse own in you veins?'

Then as later. Mamag making Son-Son so vex he dancing like a person in a tac-tac nest. 'Watch you mouth, you know! The Malheureuse family was a respectable family in the area, yes!'

And Mamag say, 'You can't talk that nonsense to people who right inside the family, to people who didn't have to read the story in book to know it. Don't tell me how respectable those Malheureuse was! And even self I swallow that dotishness, what you trying to say? Respectable blood can't bastard? Know where you come out when you talking, Son-Son. Is like you feel white blood bastard more respectable than straight black blood bastard? If you is prince then you is pauper, too. I know that, and I don't think you none the less for it, because that is my story, too. But check yourself, Mr Man.'

Son-Son vex can't done. 'Look at you!' he shouting. 'In rumshop trading word with me and dragging the Malheureuse name through the mud!'

50

'The Malheureuse name was in the mud from time,' Mamag inform him. 'How you think you manage to pick it up?' And without an ounce of shame, Mamag that day turn around to the shop and announce a toast. And is to hear toast! 'All-you, oh! Drink one for a shabin Malheureuse proud of his bastard inheritance!'

A man choke on the rum. Another one slap him on the back and ask, 'You all right dey?' People move, feeling well self-conscious. They turn away from the confusion and turn towards the counter to ask for a 'quarter' quiet like, to get another 'eighth'. Some started to drink but put the glass back down in case it might look as if they in the confusion and taking part in the toast. Family business. Is best not to put you mouth. But that kind of thing Son-Son cannot forgive. Magda has no respect for anybody. She should never have been allowed to sell that piece of land and to get so big-up with she self. He would have to see what could be done about that. Law is law.

Ti-Moun defied the notice to quit the land. Refused the offer to stay in the house on sufferance. God not sleeping, he decided. He could never lose his land just so. He kept on going to dig his yams and potatoes and pick the oranges and tend young cocoa trees. It wasn't even so much defiance. Was like Ti-Moun just didn't understand that the law had decided he didn't exist. There was no law that could do that, he was thinking. Forgetting, it look like, that is man make law to suit himself. The land was what Ti-Moun knew. His house on the land was what he know. There was nothing else. The mountain was his. Was his yesterday. Is his today. Will be his tomorrow. There is nothing else. And is not as if the land is not something he have to heart. This law could not exist.

'Leave them,' his brother Cosmos said. 'Give them their land let them swallow it make it stifle them. Don't go in the land make them kill you. Give them the land. What you fighting them for? Live and be merry, for tomorrow you die.'

But Ti-Moun explaining. 'Cosmos, is not that I setting out to fight them *per se*. Is something I work for. Is something we whole generation work for. We work up from nothing to have this. Is our land.'

'Me? I moving,' Cosmos decided. 'Nobody will make me dead for land, however much it be.'

'You moving?' Ti-Moun asked. 'Where?'

And Cosmos saying, 'Josephine have a piece she mother did leave for her down the road. We will move the house there.'

'So you letting them throw you off Papa land?' Ti-Moun was looking even kind of puzzled as he asked the question. 'Just so? After the old people work so hard on the land?'

'Boy, Ti-Moun,' Cosmos take a deep breath to answer. 'All over Paz you hearing how people killing people in this kind of confusion. Whether is because they want more or is because they feel they have to stand up for some funny kind of law, I don't know, and to tell you the truth, me brother, I don't want to know. Them is them and me is me. If they happy that way, so be it. Leave it, Ti-Moun. Me, I don't ready to dead yet. Leave the land for them, Ti-Moun. I will ask Josephine. I sure you could put up on a piece in she land, too.'

'No,' was all Ti-Moun say to this.

'But it have other road you could take,' Cosmos trying to persuade him. 'Cassandra must have a piece of land . . .'

'No,' Ti-Moun say. 'We did married already when she old man dead. Was the son of heir that inherit to share, and all girls who married he didn't give them nothing.'

52

But Cosmos had the feeling that things never complicated if you not looking for complications. He say, 'She must could get piece, Ti-Moun.'

'That would be worse confusion again,' Ti-Moun tell him. 'She brother was son-of-heir and, well, that self is another thing. The point is, I don't think it right to give up so easy. Is the principle of the thing.'

'So that is it,' Cosmos saying. 'You will kill yourself over some kind of thing you calling principle?' he asking. 'Don't study that, Ti-Moun. I could talk to Josephine. We will work something out.'

'Is all right,' Ti-Moun decide. 'Is all right. I will think of something.'

And one last plead Cosmos plead: 'Ti-Moun, leave the land for them, please. It not worth it.'

But Ti-Moun ask, 'Cosmos, what you saying? All me years, all me work, all me ideas for changing the land when I could put twopence together, all Cassandra work, all we life, all the way Papa and Mama work out they soul-case . . .'

Cosmos shrugged. Made a dry sound that might have been laughter. 'It not worth it, nuh, Ti-Moun. It just not worth it. Life too short.'

And one went one way, one the other. When Cosmos reached the corner and looked back, Ti-Moun was standing up there watching him. As he turned back, Ti-Moun self turned to go up to the mountain.

Sometimes the air is very still under the cocoa. Neither Monkey nor Crapaud saying anything. Only a few birds, using Crapaud's tune but different words, keep insisting, over and over again, as if they not referring to anything, really, that whatever happen, 'green peas sweet'.

WAIT A WHILE

Ask the cocoa leaf why its face is so wet in the early morning. Ask the breadfruit growing near the bois canot why it reaches so high. Ask Crapaud what it hears to make it keep saying, 'Wait a while'. Or listen in the night when crickets talk to the spirits that were there when cocoa, breadfruit and bois canot began their growing, when Crapaud started its croaking. Ask the little cricket why it keeps proclaiming its existence in that night-time shak-shak voice. Crick-et. Crick-et.

The child who is a toddler around the time of the maroon that moved Ti-Moun's house from the mountain to the valley grows up knowing what she sees — that a woman who speaks to no one unless she is spoken to, and even then not a lot, lives down in the flatland below Mamag's house. The woman is strange, and at one time she had a husband who was just like her. He died. People say if it hadn't been for Mamag, their little girl might have grown up dotish. But as the child grows, she knows too that nutmeg didn't begin as a brown seed in a boat with a red petticoat. It didn't even begin as a tree. Dig below the ground. And you will begin to find nutmeg's story.

The day that Ti-Moun walked away into the mountain, Crapaud's eyes were bulging above the water in the drain. No time for croaking now. No more waiting. Ti-Moun was walking in someone else's land, according to law, even if not according to life. Uncle Son-Son and his lawful nephew were standing near to a sign that read, No trespassing.

Ti-Moun remembered that the day his father married his mother, Uncle Son-Son was best man. And the four-year-old Ti-Moun knew that after Daddy, was Uncle Son-Son as man in the place. He and Cosmos used to sit down on Uncle Son-Son knee and listen to all kinds of 'nancy stories. Uncle Son-Son not stranger. They used to walk to school sometimes on a morning with Uncle Son-Son holding each one by the hand. Uncle Son-Son is family.

Monkey began to chatter when the first planass landed. Crapaud's eyes disappeared into the water when the blood began to flow. The breeze, rustling through the cocoa and nutmeg trees, sounded like rain. Crapaud heard what seemed to be running footsteps, but there was no pack of dogs and no runaway dashing into the mountains. The mountain whispered its magic to itself. And Ajakbe's mother wailed in the wind.

Cosmos, coming back from the rumshop by the crossroads and finding Cassandra worried about Ti-Moun, ventured into the land. Walking. Looking back over his shoulder. He found his brother Ti-Moun bleeding and unconscious. Carried him like a baby in his arms. A drunk man cries easily, they say, so there was no need for Cosmos to try to stop his tears. He sat on the step near to the bread and cheese plant and everybody stepped over him. Drunk as usual. And what of Ti-Moun, the careful one?

That night, it was like a wake. With reason. People came with candles and matches, with masantos filled with kerosene. Some even walked with a bottle with a little end in it, just to wet the throat. 'Look at that, eh,' people said. 'Grow up here hearing Carib talk about land confusion and about blood to come. Never thought I would see it in this Attaseat here.' Some walked with children they didn't want to leave alone in the house. You never know what these little ones could get up to. Heads covered against the dew, the girls walked inside, keeping close to their mothers. The boys sat on the big stones in the yard, picked up little stones and sent them singing through the trees into the darkness. And stories began to take shape.

'One night, eh, when my father was coming down from the mountain, he see a big ball of fire right in the corner by Mr Cosmos house there.'

'Lie!'

'Is true. All how he try to pass, the fire spreading across the road, and over in the drain, wherever he try to go.'

'And so how he reach home?'

'He cuss some bad word, nuh. Daddy say, eh, he curse, he curse, he curse and then the fire just start to fade away like.'

'And he go home?'

'Eh, well, what you think? You wouldn't have dash home fast, too?'

'All-you should have watch to see who first come and ask for matches in the morning.'

'Well, you don't think we watch, then? And . . . ' eyes look from one side to the other, voice drops to a whisper to say, 'They say was Mr Son-Son.'

Ti-Moun's face was smashed. His body was stiff and hurting. The doctor said some ribs were broken. In Trinidad, where more was known about medical things, they said, some mending might be done. Ti-Moun had taken a lot of blows in the head. But he was young enough. The body would mend.

The body mended. The eyes kept a vacant look. And what landowner would employ for cutlassing and planting a man whose fingers couldn't grip, who couldn't hold a cutlass, who couldn't see clearly enough to tell the difference between a nutmeg and a cocoa tree just by looking, who spent so much time standing as if mesmerised in the shade of the cocoa trees?

And this abomination? Hush! If is stranger is one thing. But don't put your mouth. Is family business. But is a good thing Mamag land wasn't family land. She could do as she want with it. She could get together all those who knew that it was useless to try and clap with one hand.

IN THE DIP

In the valley, the place people called The Dip, the bite of
the breeze was not the same as in the mountain. But the
hillside gave good shade. There was a maroon to finish
building the house.

'Tim! Tim!' one of the men mixing mortar shouts.

And another one come back with, 'Boy, Tim Tim the flick-
ing mortar, nuh. Make haste with the thing pass the bucket
give me.'

'Well, you don't see I doing it? Is me mouth I saying Tim
Tim with, you know. And me hand that working the spade on
the ground, yes.' And the man stands looking thoughtfully
down at the mixture on the ground, resting his hand on the
spade, wiping sweat from his forehead.

'All right,' the other person answer him, 'work it and pass
the bucket.'

'Tim! Tim!'

'But hear, nuh,' someone else interrupts, taking a nail out
of his mouth to talk, 'you saying Tim Tim there, you don't
hear what they say happen to Son-Son wife last night?'

'No. What?'

'You see him? You see this one self? Mister mix mortar with
he mouth? Mix the blasted mortar while you listening, nuh.'

'Well, you know how she like to play Christian already. Always want to help people children, and give medicine and thing? Well, she passing this day in the crossroad by the rumshop under the hill there.'

'She stop and take one?'

'Boy, behave yourself, boy. The lady is a Christian lady.'

'Well,' he passes a length of wood. Advises, 'Put this piece of stick crossways on that one.' Continues,

'Well, is late in the night, you know, and Madam Son-Son, she see a little child in the crossroad sucking the finger and scratching the belly. So she say, "Eh, but these people and them careless with their children, eh! Popo – "'

'You lie!' one mortar-mixer declares, dumping a spade-full in the bucket. 'She didn't say no *popo*. Not Madam Son-Son self. She will say . . .'

'All right. All right. She say, "Little one, what you doing there all alone at this time of night?"' The workman turn towards his audience, giving full attention to the story. He say, 'The child don't answer. Madam Son-Son move up close and she look in the child face. The eyes looking yellow, yellow and the belly punching out with the nabel. "Poor little thing!" say Mrs Son-Son. "All the signs of malnutrition." Malnutrition, she saying, *wi*. Mal-jo she mean, you know. "You need care. You need attention. Come with me and I will bring you to the doctor tomorrow. Where you living?" she trying to find out. But the child just looking poor-me-one, poor-me-one and not saying nothing. So Madam Son-Son – she very helpful in this kind of situation, you know – she pick up the little one, hoist it up on she shoulder and she walking up into the mountain, up to the amount of land they have up there, holding this poor malnourish child to bring it go by the doctor tomorrow. But she find, well, more she walk, more this child get heavy. She wondering, but she don't studying that too much, you know, she just trying to make it home. When she reach in the gap just before where Cosmos' house was there, right by the big boli tree, before you turn up the hill to Son-Son piece of land, she hear a voice from under the cocoa call out, "Ajakbe!"'

And the workman pause there, chuckling to just let the laughter go down little bit. And then he continue, 'And all of a sudden this child that she thought was so weak and so malnourish that it couldn't talk, it lift up it head and it answer, strong, strong, "Yea, Mama." Well, you could imagine! Mistress Son-Son stand up with she mouth open and she eyes swell up to fall out of she head. She root to the spot and she looking round. The voice call out again, "Ajakbe, where you dah go?" And Ajakbe answer, brisk and sprightly, "Me na know, Mama. Ce missis where da say I sick, she a bring me go doctor." Well, you could imagine! Boy, don't throw the blasted mortar mix on me foot, boy! Look you have a bucket dey! That is what it for. Mistress Son-Son drop the people child, and she gone bawling up the hill in she husband land. And the lajabless, Ajakbe mother, it down in the cocoa laughing, *kya! kya! kya! ou tini bonè-u wa!* You lucky! You well, well lucky! You shoulda hold on to me child. I woulda give you in you backside! *Kya! Kya! Kya!*'

And now Mamag voice coming in on all the merriment. 'All right! All right! Don't lie on Mistress Son-Son. I know that one already. Lajabless or no lajabless, laugh all-you laugh, but pour the mixture in let it set, eh! How all-you going?'

'All right, yes, Mamag; we should finish the whole foundation by tonight; and then three, four days, by the end of the week we could move the house.'

'Good. All-you well work. Where Cosmos? I thought he was here?'

'He was here, yes. He leave a little while now say he going out the road to come back.'

'What happen?' Mamag ask. 'Rum finish?'

'No, Mamag. We don't move through that yet, nuh. Thing not too bad. We all right. But I believe Cosmos go up the road by where they boiling to bring down another bottle.'

'Well, all-you must be hungry. All-you children, come and help carry down the food.'

'Is a oil down, Mamag?' somebody want to know.

'Mamag could cook a good oil-down, you know!' another one look up to say, rubbing his belly with a finger the colour of cement. But Mamag by now on her way to deal with the food.

At the top of the hill, Mamag turn to survey The Dip. Her eyes stay with one little girl who hasn't followed the others. 'Come, little girl,' Mamag say. 'What you stay back for? *Mu ka kiwé ou. Ou ba ka vini?*'

'Go on, girl!' a young workman shout to his sister.

The little girl learning. She challenging. But she must wait. Little child or big person, Mamag standing up to any challenge. 'Go on, little girl. You time will come.'

MEMORIES OF THE DIP

Telling the whole story of the confusion to Willive later, Mamag said, 'But, child, that was not even the end of it. Sometimes tongue only keep on talking because it know if it hush, the things it refuse to reveal could happen again. So let teeth meet with the talking and cut the thread of the wickedness.

'Child, is not everything I know. I can't say I know what talk that talk between you father and you mother under their roof. But what you hear I telling you is what I know. You say you remember me, Mamag, standing up on the hill and ordering my brother Son-Son out of my yard?

'Child, you don't know the half of it. After Son-Son and he people beat you father merciful in the land, I give him that piece in the dip there.' And Mamag chin point to The Dip. 'Son-Son decide he selling the house when Ti-Moun say he not staying in it on sufferance. He selling. Is people in the village here self put together and somebody approach Son-Son as if they buying for theyself. And is so you see the house come and buy. But not that alone. Some board too old to move, so is new lumber that have to buy to come and help build where you see all-you staying now. And who you think had tree and board selling in this area here? Was you same grand-uncle self. The same Son-Son.'

And listening to Mamag, Willive looked down towards The Dip. And long time afterwards, she couldn't remember if she actually see Uncle Son-Son walking and ordering people in The Dip that day, or if is through Mamag she remember. Because somehow the memory mix up with Mamag peeling the mace off nutmeg, and with Mamag eating mango. Uncle Son-Son directing workman in the valley under Mamag house.

But for sure was Mamag that say, 'It hurt me heart. You could imagine how it hurt me heart.'

Uncle Son-Son like a real jefe, dropping board and sand. Telling people what to do and with a pencil behind his ears. Putting his hand on his waist and looking around.

And for sure too was Mamag that say, 'In me land, yes. Looking around as if he mean all these and those are mine. That is the quality of my brother and my sister Isidora and the other one that they say is my nephew. That is family! That is law! Child, mother may have, father may have, but God bless the child that hath his own. Child, take what I telling you. Don't pick up idea of family put on your account. You is you own and you only person in this world. Not friend, not family. Is you. If family and friend turn out good, is a bonus. Enjoy it. But don't expect it. Child, Willive, listen to me good. Me, Mamag, talking to you here. If you think I nice to you today, that good. But don't expect it. Expect that I could turn viper tomorrow. Don't trust not a soul, child. Not one living soul. And always tell anybody close to you, any child God might grant you in the future, what is the colour of blood, how it flow and who it is that cut the skin to see it flow.'

And Willive remembers, too, that she wanted to cry. Mamag might turn viper tomorrow.

Willive has in her mind this picture of people holding their belly and bawling for what happen. But must be through what Mamag say. Or people hold their belly and bawl for true? Because Mamag say is only because people use the eyes God give them for seeing and not just for decoration, that the village was able to build the house back for Ti-Moun and Cassandra. 'People round here put their one and two pence together as if was their own mother children. The house that is my brother Mayum and he children property fair and square. You ever see a thing like that? Me is their precious Malheureuse, too, but child, you hear? Is *stranger* that put their hand and their head together, that help make it possible for your father to make a living. He own blood make him eat the very bread that the devil knead.'

And Willive just stayed quiet that time when Mamag was talking, taking in the story to pass on as a lesson. The song in her head that time was one she heard in a maroon once:

Mooma, Mooma
Your son in the gaol already
Your son in the gaol already
Your son in the gaol already
Tie a kerchief and ban you belly.

'Child,' Mamag said, 'every story have a long tail. The plainest story is only a little part of the riddle.'

Alone in her bed the night after Mamag told her the story, Willive cried for a long time before sleep came to hush her. And what you believe she thinking? How Mamag might turn viper tomorrow.

The family go through a lot, but Willive, people said, couldn't possibly remember. She was too young then. But she did remember. Perhaps what she recalled was partly what her mother recalled, but after the confusion her mother said little, although the child could hear her crying at night. So perhaps what she remembered was what she heard in her mother's sobbing and in her silences. Or it may have been what her father recalled, but Ti-Moun had been reduced to silence, so perhaps it was really what Mamag, her grandaunt, painted for her, because Mamag remembered it all. And the thing is that later, many who weren't there remembered, too. Remembered especially that Carib had spoken long before, and that the prophecy had come to pass.

What Willive always told Mamag was that she had a vivid memory of one August afternoon in the valley.

Mamag remembered that those August days were so hot that Willive's mother Cassandra made bakes in the big flat iron pot on the fireside outside the house instead of baking bread in the oven. Fire on top, fire below, to cook the bakes, but less heat than standing in front of the big oven. And still the days were getting hotter.

Willive toddled around, that August afternoon, in The Dip, below Mamag's house, where they were staying while their own house was being built. Cassandra had taken the bakes out of the pan and was sitting on the rocking-chair inside, looking at Ti-Moun stretched out on the bed. Son-Son was selling board in The Dip and children were passing over the hill from the track.

The part that Willive really remembers is stooping down there in The Dip, scratching where the sandflies bit her and looking up at Mamag. Arms akimbo, Mamag had planted herself in front of the mango tree on the hill. Her face was the brown of the cocoa trees around her. The yellow and red pattern of her headtie was like the red mace petticoat of the nutmeg peeping from the pod. Miss Nancy Etticoat, as the saying goes, in a red petticoat. Mamag was looking down at the activity in The Dip.

'*Bonjay!*' she shouted, raising her face to the blue.

'*Bonjay!*' arms akimbo and eyes fixed on the valley below. 'Look at that! Look at this in the open here. Where you see people playing about in their mess, is to leave them there in truth. Because play you play with puppy, it will lick you mouth. Son-Son was like a chupidee growing up, fraid people like what and couldn't talk to save his life. Is he brother and mine, the same Mayum Malheureuse those children father self, that hold Son-Son hand day in day out put word in he mouth like food, feed him with answer for word like gravy. And look at that now, eh, *mem cozé Mayum ba-i Son-Son, Son-Son pwan-i y lagay-la com yu woche sous tête mamay Mayum*. Play with puppy, puppy sure to lick food out of you mouth.'

Son-Son exploded. The children on their way up through the track, going up from the Thursday meeting in the church-hall, spilled out from the track behind the house with their mouths open, their faces questioning the commotion in the yard.

Voices climbed over each other:

'What do? I wonder what do? What Mamag shouting so for? You understand what she saying?'

And one explaining to the other, 'She saying that Son-Son was like a chupidee growing up and was he brother Mayum that teach him to talk, now Son-Son taking the same word Mayum put in he mouth to come and let go like big stone on Mayum children head.'

Willive's eyes moved from the figure of her grandaunt

Mamag on the hill to her granduncle Son-Son, trapped in The Dip.

The children were caught in mid-flight. Fingers tore a leaf apart. A hand pulled at the skirt of a hurrying friend.

'Wait, nuh? Don't go yet.' Feet wanted to go home but bodies kept turning back, pulling them around to dilly-dally in The Dip. 'Thing happening,' they whispered, 'thing happening. We can't go yet. Wait let us see.'

And meanwhile Son-Son was dancing with rage. 'Mayum was my lawful brother,' he shouted. 'My lawful brother. One mother, one father. So watch you mouth! The Lord know the right and the wrong of it. Is the lawful way.' Uncle Son-Son walked, turned, walked back.

On the hill, Mamag was triumphant. 'Yes,' she shouted. *Wi.* Stay there. *Mwen métté-u la. Wété la.* The truth well tie you there. Is me that put you there. Stay there.'

'Is the law.' Son-Son threw the words right across the nutmeg trees that were planted all around at the time. 'Is the law. God self see is only justice and the law.'

And it was as if that law word turned Mamag's whole inside upside down. She walked up and down, up and down, on the hill and pointed down into The Dip at Son-Son. 'Take out God from your mouth, Satan. You think God is dotish people? If you read God word with any sense in your head, you would have no mouth to talk. Nation shall rise against nation, is the warning, and family against family. And as for the law, let me teach you the scripture, Son-Son, you and your law that you bringing out to kick your brother children that he say is his out of house and home because he dead and you say them is bastard. Who is you? Who is law? I spit on your law! Luke 20, verse 46, Mr Son-Son: Be on your guard against the teachers

74

of the Law, who like to walk around in their long robes and love to be greeted with respect in the market-place; who choose the reserved seats in the synagogues and the best places at feasts; who take advantage of widows and rob them of their homes, and then make a show of saying long prayers! Their punishment will be all the worse!'

And Mamag stood on the hill with her arms akimbo and spat on the ground for emphasis. The children's excitement was running high. You should hear them.

'Woy! Mamag good eh! All-you don't hear Mamag quote scripture? She quote the Bible flush, you know! All-you don't hear?'

'That is the same passage the priest read in church, word for word.'

'How you know? You know Bible?'

'I remember, yes. Ah sure, sure. Mamag good for he Mr Son-Son.'

And who know if is because somebody lean too hard against the counter that Son-Son put up across two planks of wood for conducting his business that it fall, or if is because Mamag's words just lean too heavy in the wind? People jump aside when the counter crash, children scattering and laughing, but they waiting, and watching, because Mamag still talking on the hill.

'The Good Book have a straight passage just for you, my brother. Papa God watching. Let the truth tie you right there! But in fact self, get out!'

And now Mamag had changed her mind. She put one foot forward down the hill, balancing on a little rock, and pointing with one finger to emphasise her decision.

'You trespassing on my land!' she shouted at Son-Son. 'Go! *Alé*, before I put the same law in you skin.'

Uncle Son-Son stumbled out of the yard, shouting, stuttering: 'Shame! Shame! Don't think I don't know is the same family money that buy the land you showing off with there!'

And Mamag shouting back: 'Shame? Is shame all right. Family money? All who want to say them is family must come and confront me to talk. I have no loupgarou family. Not one ounce of blood-sucking family I have. Is the Malheureuse bad-blood that fly up in you head! Keep me out of it.'

And Mamag turned away, walking through the nutmeg trees to her house right up there in the curve of the hillside.

The children's feet turned slowly away. They didn't want to go. You could hear from the talk how they enjoyed it all.

'All-you don't hear? Loupgarou family, yes. Mamag call Son-Son loupgarou! Boy, that is jokes here today, yes. Joan, ent that is all you family, too? You in the loupgarou family? Joan!'

'Girl, don't be stupid, girl. Who you talking to?'

'Who I talking to? How you mean? You in the family, yes. Ent you grandfather is their cousin? But in fact self, don't study me, nuh. My mother side is that same family. And you, too, Constance, because you mother and my mother is relative, so you better don't say nothing.'

'My mother say everybody related to everybody in this village here, so none of us can't talk.'

Their eyes keep checking behind to make sure nothing starting again. But nothing was starting. Was just the ending for now. Son-Son walking away cursing words children shouldn't hear. And the children of course giggling. One of the grown-ups called out. 'Hey! Children! Pull all-you tail home and don't stand up down here interfering in big people business! Home!'

The children scampered away, and you could see a dress-band

trailing, a ribbon flying, shirt-tail drooping. Giggling. Someone chanted, longmouth, longteeth/newsmonger creepcreep, but the big people were too far away to hear. The Dip was quiet again.

When Willive peeped around the door, Ti-Moun was sitting on the bed, with his head in his hands. Her mother, Cassandra, was sitting on the chair near to the bed, over by the washstand, looking down at the floor. The silence frightened the child. She ran back outside, out on to the step to hug up Mamag and hide her face in her skirt.

People say she was too young, really, to remember anything, but she remembered a lot from that Thursday in August. She remembered Mamag and Uncle Son-Son. She remembered how her father Ti-Moun sat on the bed with his head in his hands. She remembered the way her mother sat on the chair near to the bed, looking at the floor. And for some reason she remembered the washstand standing there in the corner, and the silence covering everything.

Mamag and The Dip

If you look at the cocoa pod on the tree, you will notice how sometimes it grows right in the curve of the branch, in the place where the branch bends from the weight of the cocoa. Mamag's house was like that. It looked like it had grown in the curve of the hillside. The house sat comfortably in the curve of the hillside, backed up against the rock. When you leave the main road, walk through the track and get to where Mamag's house was, there was nowhere else to go. You came slap bang against the rock.

In those days, after the move to The Dip, Willive was mostly at Mamag's house. Willive's mother, Cassandra, spoke little in those days. And Ti-Moun, her father, was quiet as death.

Strange. Willive could remember that day with Mamag on the hill and Granduncle Son-Son dancing like a person in a tac-tac nest. She could remember the room in Mamag's house and her mother and father sitting there, but her father's death, and details around the funeral, remained a blank. What she knew about that was what Mamag told her over the years. How Ti-Moun had had to go to Trinidad a second time after that initial visit and had returned only to die. As far as Willive remembers, one time he was there and all of a sudden he wasn't there. She doesn't remember an event that was his death. Or even his funeral.

Willive was a sombre child, growing up. Kind of cagoo, people said. Into herself, like. Until she was thirteen, she sucked on her thumb and often had her hand pulling at one of the soft plaits into which Mamag usually braided her hair. Always thinking and looking far away. As if she could remember a time when things had promised to be different and that the promise had died without warning.

It was Mamag's stories that eventually weaned her away from the thumb and turned her eyes more often towards the mountain, watching how the clouds covered the blue behind there, and how the blue always struggled through again. But even after she stopped sucking the thumb, sometimes she would just sit down looking at it, as if she missed it and wasn't sure where the good taste of it had gone, or what to use in its place.

'Fix your face, child,' Mamag would say, touching a plait with gentle fingers. 'Take the finger out of your mouth. You looking like nobody child. Come let Mamag hug you up.'

And sometimes, when they sat taking out the mace, Mamag started a song. To Willive, the tune was like her school song, Mary Had a Little Lamb, with different words:

Down in the valley
Two by two
Two by two
Two by two
Down in the valley two by two
Rise, Sally, rise.

Let me see you make a motion
Two by two

Two by two
Two by two
Let me see you make a motion
Two by two
Rise, Sally, rise.

'When you see the world knock you down,' Mamag would say, flinging the mace on to the crocus bag spread out on the floor, 'is to get up and square up for the battle.'

And she would stretch her mouth out, the bottom lip longer than the top one. Her chin would be full of little long lines all of a sudden. But all the time her hands would be gentle on the mace, prising the petals away from the brown nutmeg without breaking them.

'Square up for the battle,' she would unfold her lips to say again, flinging more mace on to the crocus bag and then pushing the spectacles further up on her nose. 'These people they don't make spectacles for my kind of nose. When you buy the spectacles, they expect you to buy nose support along with it. Child, square up for the battle. The world not nice. Sometimes things good, but most times it bad. And if you don't decide to square up for the battle, you might as well turn you back on Papa God world right from the beginning.

'You hearing me? Is not everything, everything people must say to children, but you getting big. Yes, you getting big.'

And once she said, 'Twelve years you having this Christmas coming. Twelve! Young lady. And your mother, well, life didn't treat her too nice. She take my poor brother son put on her account there, and, well . . .'

And sometimes Mamag would just go silent, her eyes and

hands occupied with the mace, her teeth pulling the top lip down so far that her bottom lip was up there right under the nose.

And she would say again, 'Is not everything, everything people must tell children, but you have to know some things. You must know what happen in long time days, so you will expect the rough with the smooth, and it won't knock you down when it come. Because the rough will come. As sure as Mohammed went to the mountain, it coming, and you have to know how to turn you hand and box you brains to settle yourself in this world.'

Sometimes the way how Mamag talked Willive couldn't help trying to tease her. When she talked about boxing brains, Willive turned her hand around and around, looked at it intently and then slapped her hand against her head. 'I boxing me brains, yes, Mamag.' Mamag didn't laugh. She just cut her eyes. But Willive giggled. She knew Mamag was amused.

'Mohammed went to the mountain, Mamag?' Willive asked in a low voice when Mamag still didn't speak. 'I thought they say the mountain went to Mohammed in the end, Mamag?'

And Mamag, pretending to be annoyed, answered, 'You hear you? Ants like you, you don't even know your name yet, but you trading word with me.'

'I know my name, yes, Mamag. Is Willive is my name.'

'You know the sound of your name, Madam Willive. The sound of your name you know. But you trading word with me. You trading word, yes, little Ti-Moun, so you don't see is right for you to know the meaning of the words you trading? It right for you to know.'

And that time Mamag was silent for a long, long time, dipping into her bosom for the handkerchief with her change, taking it out, untying it, counting, putting it back down inside there and sitting back to look up at the rafters, at how the smoke from the kitchen had curled in through the door and blackened them. Willive slapped at the rain flies that fluttered every so often against her legs. They couldn't reach Mamag through the folds of her frock and petticoat. The child went closer so that the frock could shield her, too.

'Everything that happening today,' Mamag said at last, 'it happen before. Is a true, true word. Thing changing, you know. Thing changing. A lot of thing different. But, child, there is nothing new under the sun. When the rain set up in the mountain there, we look and we say, rain coming, and we rush and pick up the one-one cocoa on the ground, we pull the mace inside fast for it not to wet and rot, we pick up the two piece of clothes on the fence. And then when the rain pour down now, everything inside. That good. You prepare. But sometimes you don't even see the rain set up. Sun shining like crazy, and awhoosh! Sudden shower. You stand up with your mouth open. If you prepare already for anything, you mouth might still open with the first shock, but you don't leave it open too long to catch fly. You run and you turn you hand to something, pick up everything before it get too wet, then when sun come out again now, two-twos you back on course. You back on course.'

And Mamag would be quiet for a long time again. The way Mamag talked, Willive could imagine ships sailing like in the pictures in the reading book. Ships going off course and coming back on course.

'Your mother and your father, God rest his soul, it hit them hard,' Mamag said. 'They know nation shall rise against nation, and father against child, and family against family, and they

85

know about nation divided against itself. But in their mind they thinking, other nation, other family. When it happen right inside here self, right inside the family yard, it still shock them. Strong as they is, bold and brave as they is, all what they know from time, it break them. It break them. Truth to tell, child, it could break anybody. It could break anybody.'

And Mamag wiped a speck of dust from the corner of her eye. And hummed for a little while. *Rise, Sally, Rise.* 'Your father get such a shock he dead and gone one lick. From heartbreak. Your mother is nothing like she old self. She was woman with a lotta life in she days. *Gadé, matnu*, she there like she not there. Heartbreak. But, child, if you always prepare for the worst, even from people you think you know like the palm of your hand, from me and everybody you think you know, the world will bend you but it won't break you. The load will never be too heavy. Never be too heavy.'

Willive looked at Mamag. The worst from Mamag? She wouldn't get the worst from Mamag. She wanted to ask her to make sure: 'You mean you too, in truth, Mamag?' But Mamag was talking again, and Willive didn't want to interrupt.

'Child, yesterday is today, is tomorrow, is the day after. You must know. You not too young. You not too young at all. Is long, long time Carib telling us what is to happen. But we never expect nothing to happen to us, and because she not talking the same way as us, we think she stupid. Child, you must learn from that and listen.

'The little Carib, now, who born in the mental asylum, me daughter in town just take her to stay with her. But she head is all for coming back in the cocoa where she mother and she grandmother was. And the spirit with her. She talking now about blood. Blood, she saying, to come in the south. Is she talking but is not she. She saying thing she know nothing about. When the spirit leave her and you talking with her, you wonder if is the same person. Little girl, like any little girl. She going to school, but I know she won't stay for long because the others teasing her all the time. Child, always listen. The spirit more than the person. Listen to everybody like them or not. And pick sense from nonsense. Yesterday is today.'

And while Mamag talked, a big bottle-fly got trapped in the curtain and stayed there buzzing until the noise unsettled Mamag so much that she eased up off the chair and stretched across to push the window open and shake out the curtain to release it. Released, the bottle-fly didn't leave, but stayed there on the window, quiet. And Mamag said, 'This one must be somebody visiting. Somebody visiting, when you see that.'

And it was then that Willive remembered, all of a sudden, her father Ti-Moun lying down on the bed with his eyes closed. Was after he came back from Trinidad. She didn't know how she knew that, but she knew. And wasn't long. As if wasn't long.

And years afterwards the two things were mixed up in her mind. Mamag talking, the bottle-fly on the window, and Ti-Moun lying down with his eyes closed. And she Willive standing by the bed watching him. Daddy? Daddy? But Daddy didn't answer, and Willive went out and closed the door quiet, quiet. And walked out to the barrier to stand up and watch her mother putting up stick for the tomato plant that coming up.

Mamag talked about getting old, and about the way people talked about old, old people who seemed to be losing their ordinary senses as if they were in a second childhood. Mamag said, 'And you know, they saying second childhood as if is a thing to pity. People, eh. They know so much that they know nothing at all. Second childhood. What you think it is? Is just that some don't forget yet and some just starting to remember. Second childhood, is what they call it.' And Mamag hush for a while, and Willive thinking, *Must have been after that that I open the door again and see Uncle Cosmos by the bed and hear him saying, 'Ti-Moun? Ti-Moun, say something, nuh.' And Daddy eyes still close. 'Ti-Moun?'*

Mamag saying, 'What happen, child? You all right? What happen, *dous-dous*? You head hurting you? Shift little bit. Shift. Let Mamag wash she mango hand and hug you up. Second childhood. Child, sometimes in this second childhood people could hear the howling that come like a warning in the night clearer than those that lose their first childhood and not seeing their second one yet. Child, second childhood is not a disgrace.'

And while Mamag was talking, the wind got trapped in the corner behind the house. And stayed there for a while, whistling and howling. And Willive thinking, *For sure was after that that Mammy say, 'You uncle Cosmos say he going in Trinidad, yes. He say he going.' For sure was after. Because was after . . .* But Willive couldn't remember. Although she could remember her mother saying, that whole parcel of children. A whole parcel of children, yes. Or was Mamag that say that afterwards? Or . . . ? And Willive didn't know anything any more. Was a lot of years, and she was a baby, really. So perhaps she was only imagining. And Willive was anxious to hear Mamag's story now, and waiting for her to talk.

And Mamag talked. That day and the day after and the next one after that. And what Mamag couldn't talk, the way how she told it Willive weave a story from the threads she get from the talking. And when later she passed it on, was a story that

Mamag told, is true, but was also a story that the wind told when Mamag paused to consider. Was a story that the wind repeated again at night when Willive slept and her mind took the time to play with the loose threads of Mamag's words. Was a story that the night sounds like the cricket voices told when darkness made Willive pull the sheet right over her head and lie down there trembling and afraid. Was a story that time told.

THUNDER

From early on, when Mamag saw the way Willive's little boy cowered in a corner at the sound of thunder, she said, 'Children fraid thunder is true. But this one not ordinary fraid. It look like it have something in the mortar than just the pestle. Must be something from another life that he remember.' Mamag already. As if one life not enough to deal with.

But it was that comment that made Willive laugh and remind Mamag of something that she had told her long time. 'Funny you should say that. Is forgetful you getting forgetful, but you remember how I tell you long time that my mother used to sit down on the bed when she remembering far back and talk about some long-ago ancestor of ours that they kill in the market in Paz City on a night when it had a lot of thunder? From what Mammy say they beat him in his head and he lie down in the market-square in town bleeding to death. And I always remember her shaking her head and saying, was a miserable night, yes. Was a night full of rain just the same way. Was a night with thunderstorm. And she say that where they kill him was under a shop-front, and they leave him there, lying down under the awning, with blood all over his face and thunder making raymabuddy.'

And Mamag say, 'You right, chile. That is the connection. And that is where your story and the Malheureuse story cross. Is that he remembering. You know that. Lord have is mercy! One kill the other and so now Thunder have murderer and victim inside of his head. And even in we time, the story don't really change. Lord have is mercy!'

And Mamag made the sign of the cross and continue, 'You know, somehow I never really think and put the two thing together. Just wasn't time, perhaps. Willive, don't take that light, nuh, child. Yesterday is today is tomorrow. And sure as day that is what the boy have in his head.' Mamag made the sign of the cross again, and Willive laughed a nervous laugh.

Laugh but still buy a candle to put in the church and that was when, at Mamag's advice, she took Thunder along to hear what Carib had to say. She watched him more closely after that. Listened with trembling to his wail of thunder, mama, thunder. After all, who know what is what?

Once, the children in Thunder's school started a story about how when thunder rolling was God up there vex and throwing thunderbolt behind Christ. After that, whenever he heard thunder, he ran to her and hid his face in her skirts, crying, 'Thunder-Christ, mama. Thunder-Christ.' It was one of the children who started calling him Thunder, mocking his fear, and the name had stuck. Willive thought at first that this might even help, forcing him to confront what he was afraid of. He didn't seem to mind the name, but it didn't help his fear.

In the middle of all the terror he carried inside, Willive was glad that he had both Mamag and Cassandra to talk to when he was little. He was impatient and fretting with them sometimes, but she was sure it did him good.

Sometimes Mamag would say to Thunder, 'Sh-h-h! Listen. Listen.' And he would sit there with her listening to nothing. Nothing, that is, but the sound of the wind in the trees. Sometimes he would get really vex because he didn't hear anything, but Mamag was always pleased that he had listened.

Mamag was always like that, leaving you with things to unwrap in your mind. When Thunder was about eight years old and went up to Mamag's house one day after school, he stood looking at the house how it was tucked away there in the corner of the hill. 'Mamag,' he said, 'your house is the last one in the line. Nowhere else to go after that.' And Mamag, leaning on her stick, watched him from the top of the steps. Then she start walking down the steps, saying, 'I could manage,' when he tried to hold her hand to help her. 'It slow, but I could manage. Come. I want to show you something.'

Moving one today, one tomorrow, because her legs weren't strong, you know, Mamag walked to the back of the house. Past the mango tree, peering up into the lime tree, muttering, 'Me eyes don good. I can't even see what the lime tree saying.' And they walked past the kitchen join up with the house on the right and the fowl run on the left, walked slap up against the rock. There Mamag stop and say, 'Watch, little Ti-Moun. Come.'

Lift her stick and lean forward to push back the branches of a peas tree plant there to the left of the rock. 'You see that, *petit garçon*? That track, people don't use it for a long time. But it there. It take you right down into the road on the other side. You could go down there and if you turn left under the thick bush down there, you coming out right under the old mill where those African people that still walking around used to grind the sugar cane and make sugar in the old days.

The same mill where they still boiling rum and where we getting molasses from in the cane season. And if you go straight down, you coming out right in the road down in the bottom. Right out in the clear. This same jookootoo track you see here. Bringing you out by all those places. It have nowhere else to go?' And Mamag chuckle deep down in her throat. 'It always have somewhere else to go, Ti-Moun. You could bet you last half-crown, it will always have somewhere else to go.'

Mamag saved her breath as she walked back, one today, one tomorrow. Sat down on the big flat step at the bottom and rest little bit before taking the climb back up again. And Thunder meantime was looking up into the branches of the mango tree, searching for ripe ones. 'I see this place change. I live through three and even four generations, God be praised. *Petit garçon*, tell people the colour of mud, how it does be when it dry and what happen when rain come. Study you book, but life sense is not book sense, so study you head. Watch up there how the sky so blue, but you hear what Carib saying only yesterday when she come up the hill here? The blue crying red. Blood gone and blood to come, and is people like you, that know the story of the life of the land, that have to stop the red from taking over. Help me inside, you hear, *petit garçon*. Help me inside.'

And there was Thunder's grandmother Cassandra, who sat in her rocking chair when she wasn't stretched out on the bed. She would lean forward in her chair and look at him and say, 'Ti-Moun. Ti-Moun, it will be all right this time.' And sometimes she would say, all of a sudden, 'Oh! Oh! Ti-Moun, you close the back door?'

When he tried to explain, 'Grannie, my name is William. Not Ti-Moun,' she would look as if she wanted to cry. 'Will,' she would say. 'Will.' And she would just bow her head and sit down there in the rocking-chair by the window looking at the floor and every so often muttering 'Will, Will'. And once she looked at him and said, 'Where Cosmos? Cosmos self just disappear? Where Cosmos?' And another time, 'Is not today day. The funny side. Hold up you head. John Bull. John Bull.'

One morning, when Willive opened the door to call Cassandra, she found her mother sitting at the window, her head resting on the window sill. She had died looking down into The Dip where years ago Son-Son had put up the make-shift counter to sell his lumber.

It had all happened a long time ago, but before Willive called anybody, she sat down on the bed looking at the washstand and the rocking-chair in the corner and cried for the happiness her mother had lost so early. That was the Sunday. When, on the Friday of that week, Carib came and stood up there in The Dip singing 'When the roll is called up yonder', Willive thought it was in tribute to her mother. At first. But when she heard the racket the dogs made with their howling that night, she made the sign of the cross and said to herself, 'It look like somebody else going, yes.'

Perhaps Carib was paying a tribute to Cassandra, too. But for sure she was announcing the departure of Mamag, who had been like a mother to her. When, at the age of thirteen, the little girl had gone back to her mother's place in the cocoa under the Anglican church, it was Mamag who looked out for her. And those in Content who might otherwise have troubled her, left her alone, knowing that she was Mamag's charge and having real respect for Mamag and her mouth.

Willive saw Carib climb the hill to Mamag's house and

followed. 'She batting,' Willive said, and sent a message by the bus driver for the youngest of Mamag's daughters, the only one still in Paz, in Paz City, to come up to her mother. She went out to the Post Office, too, and made a telephone call to the store in town. They sat with Mamag that night and she recognised no one. Just stared vacantly and kept talking about going to the river.

No one seemed to know Mamag's age for sure, but she was certainly almost a hundred. A lot of runs for one person to make. Early the Saturday morning, Mamag close her eyes and the breath rattle in her throat. Carib kneel down there at the bedside and with tears in her eyes, she say in a quiet voice, 'Sing a joyful song. Mamag, my footstep, she walking away. It hard to see the body go, but Mamag go be able to say a word for us. Mamag going to glory. And she staying with us to lead us to glory.'

Together Carib and Willive sang 'When the roll is called up yonder'. And it was Carib who walked up and down Content, way up to Attaseat and back, singing the news of Mamag's death in the old way. Putting in even more than was absolutely necessary. Giving the whole story of Mamag's generation. '*Sa ki tan palé lut!* Mamag – Ma Magdalene Malheureuse *alé oh!* Mother of four in Trinidad and one in Paz City *alé, oh!* Content Village, Mamag *alé oh!*'

And that time, with Mamag gone like that, Willive thought about her Uncle Cosmos, who people say disappear in Trinidad right after his brother dead, just disappear and never look back. Willive wonder about him, if he alive or dead, and hope that whatever happen with him, he have somebody to give him some cold water in the end. A restless soul, Mamag had said about him once. A restless soul. Poor thing, I hope he meet it all right and prepare himself enough here for the next one. And now Willive found herself thinking: With Mamag gone now, he go be all right.

Thunder self was just past his tenth birthday when Mamag kicked the bucket, when she went, as Mamag herself would have said, to travel some place else. And Thunder was afraid, because he knew Mamag wasn't really gone, and he hoped he would never see her. He used to pull the covers over his head and hope not to hear when Mamag's voice spoke through howls in the night, or through the crickets singing in the darkness.

'Mammy,' he asked his mother one night, 'what will happen if Mamag come back?'

'It is finished, son. Mamag not coming back.'

'But her spirit, Mammy. What will happen if . . . ?'

'You won't see her, son. Mamag spirit is good spirit. And think about it. If even Mamag could come back, she know how frightened you would be, she would never do that to you. Mamag not coming back. Nothing to fraid.' That helped a little. Thunder was still afraid, especially on rainy nights, but he knew Mamag wouldn't do anything to frighten him and he gradually became more confident that she would make sure not to appear to him.

Thunder had a way he used to talk about grey days and blue days. Any day that was a rainy day was a grey day. Lucky for him, most days were bright, with the sky blue, blue and clean, clean. Those were his blue days. Willive used to watch him from the window where she sat at her sewing machine.

Even the blue days were treacherous sometimes, though. Not a cloud in the sky, behind the mountain showing not the least sign of rain and all of a sudden thunder crashing like crazy out of a clear blue sky. A really clear sky, mind you, a sky like a blue sheet tucked down behind the mountain without a crumple.

Sometimes, on both blue days and grey days, but especially on grey days when he was afraid to be at home alone, Thunder would go after school to meet Willive at the Nutmeg depot, which everyone called the Nutmeg Pool, where she worked. Sometimes he wanted to help her separate the first-grade mace from the second-grade. But Willive would shout at him.

'Don't put you hand in that damn thing.'

And he would say, 'But, Mammy, I know which is which.'

But that didn't seem to please her. She would say, 'I don't care what you know. You know? Who tell you? You better study you book and don't full up you head with stupidness. You ever see I make you stoop down and separate mace? Watch the colour. You see it? That is how it living. By sucking me blood. Is a blasted loupgarou, you hear me? It sucking my blood. I don't want it take yours.'

And the women who were sitting down there in a circle with her, with trays of red mace on their laps, bags of mace on the ground near to them and bags of nutmegs in the open corridor nearby, said, 'Damn right, too. It get enough of we blood already.' And one of them might say something like, 'I telling my little one that, he playing he head harden. Damn right, too. If you coming in here, come as he so,' and the woman would push her chin out and point at the man walking around in a white shirt and grey pants. 'You see he? He is office man. Black like me, yes. Not even brown. But office man. He only does come here now and then to see how things going. Study you book and come as he. Don't come as we. And you hair little soft already from the Indian in you father, so you could make good quick. Study you head and come as he.'

And Willive would look at her son from out under her eyelashes, as if to say, 'I hope you listening.'

Thunder was listening. Sometimes, when they refused to let him help, he wanted to go home. At times he even went, if it was a weekday. On a Friday, though, he always stayed, because his father might be home and he didn't like it much when his father was home. His father never had much to say. He worked as a bell-boy in a hotel in Paz City and came up on a Friday.

No. Ned, Willive's husband, was not a talker. To Thunder it seemed that he either didn't talk at all, or he was fretting about something or the other. Willive usually washed on a Friday night, in the tub behind the house, and put out the clothes on the lines in the fowl-run, because the fowls would be locked up inside the coops. Or sometimes she would wash on a Saturday morning in the river. And occasionally, if there was no work in the Pool, she would go to the river on a weekday. But mostly she washed on a Friday or Saturday because of Ned. That was when he came up with his dirty clothes.

Most times when Thunder went to meet Willive in the Nutmeg Pool, she would ask him, 'You do all right in school today?'

And he would answer, 'Yes, Mammy.'

And Willive would say, 'Good. You is me future.'

And the woman who sat next to her sorting the mace used to say, 'You is all of we future. All-you young people, you is this country future. All of us future.'

Thunder would watch the red, shiny mace and want to touch. He didn't dare. He would watch it and he could hear his mother's voice inside his head saying, touch it if you bad. He knew she would slap him right there in front of everybody.

So he just used to stand up there, looking at the mace, watching his mother and her friends with their heads bent down over the sorting, their shoulders curved over the trays of red.

Thunder liked school before scholarship time, that is, before the years when he was studying for the scholarship that would get him into High School, and after, when he went down to town and went to High School at the Catholic Boys' College. But later on he said that the scholarship year was one of the worst memories of that period of his life.

Willive had told him, 'I want to try and get you into that school.' To tell you the truth, at the time she said the name of the school, really, but Thunder's memory wouldn't hold that. The name by which most people called the school was also the name of the headmaster, and up to today, years later, Thunder still wouldn't call that name.

So what he remembered was that Willive said, 'I want to get you into that school. Every year he taking all the scholarships. Everybody who pass through there sure to get scholarship even if they have salt in their head. And I know you don't have salt in yours. I want to get you into that school.'

Thunder was so afraid of the reputation of that headmaster that he answered, 'But they say he does beat a lot, Mammy.'

'Is not the beating, son,' Willive said. 'Is what you get out of it. If a little beating will sort out you whole future, take the beating, me son. You mother don't have nothing, you father don't have nothing. To exist in this world, you have to get you own. And this is the only way I know to give it to you. Take a little beating today and live in comfort tomorrow. Take the beating, child.'

The headmaster said he was full. It was only a small school, he said. He couldn't take any more. People had booked up for years before. And he had taken some extras, even. The class was bursting at the seams. Thunder was overjoyed.

But Willive said, 'Please, sir, take him for me. If even is a chair you put right next to you in front, take him. Give him a future for me. Take him.'

The headmaster sighed, scratched his head and said, 'You-all make it so hard. All right. All right. Bring him. Send him when school open.'

When school started, things looking bright. Thunder found that he was in scholarship class, yes, but in a class run by some-one else, not the headmaster. For a few days, he managed to avoid questions from his mother by being too busy eating, or running outside to play with his friends, or just answering in a roundabout way.

One afternoon, as he was rushing past her up the steps, his mother said, 'Stand up there, Mister man. Thunder, you not in same class with Calvin? Calvin mother say you not in same class with him. What is this? You not in scholarship class?'

And Thunder explained, 'Just that it have more than one scholarship class, Mammy.'

'Which class you in?'

'Miss Johnson class.'

And Willive said, 'That no good. Is the man that getting the passes. I want you in his class.'

Thinking of the strap that the boys said the headmaster soaked in strong pee every night to keep it supple, Thunder argued, 'Is the same thing, Mammy. Is the same thing, you know.'

But Willive insisted, 'Is not the same thing at all.'

The next morning, Willive went to the school with him. To say, 'Sir, I want him in your class. Is the only reason I send him here, so he could get the benefit of your direct attention, sir. I want him with you, not with anybody else.'

The headmaster said, 'Miss Johnson is a good teacher, Madam.'

But Willive had an answer to that: 'I don't doubt that, sir. I don't doubt that at all. I have nothing to say against Miss Johnson. I just don't know. But with you, sir, I know. And is where a person confidence is. And is the future for this little boy who have nothing else in the world I concern about. If I drop down tomorrow, I want to be able to feel sure that I do the best I could do for him.'

The headmaster sighed and said, 'It hardly have room to stick a pin in that classroom now.'

Willive explained, 'He will be like a common pin, sir, not a safety pin. You just have to find a pinpoint to stick him in.'

And then the headmaster smiled, actually smiled. For the first and only time Thunder could remember. Smiled and then folded up his lips and frowned and looked embarrassed about smiling. 'You very determined, Ma'am. OK. Come to my class, young man.'

A chair had been placed for Thunder almost at the headmaster's elbow. There was no other room, really. No room even for the headmaster to walk comfortably up and down between all the rows. But that didn't stop him. Those who couldn't get their beating on the spot for not knowing the answers had to stay after class when there would be more room.

Thunder didn't have that problem. He was easy to reach with the strap, and the strap reached him often. For the next eight months until the scholarship exams, Thunder cried every morning when he woke up and realised that he had to go to school. Willive was sorry. She didn't like to see him like that.

'Take me out of the school, then, Mammy,' Thunder begged when she dried his tears and told him she wanted him to be happy.

But she pleaded with him, too. 'Listen, son. Is for your own good. You think I want to see you unhappy and crying like this? But this is the man that getting the scholarships and he will put you in line to sort out you future. I sorry, son. I really sorry because I don't like to see you unhappy. But take in everything he telling you, OK? It will soon be over. The beating is only for a time. Is the future that important. You think I want to be slaving my life out every day going in the Nutmeg Pool and sitting down behind a tray choosing mace? But look at it this way, child. We don't have a acre of land to we name, not one quarter acre, even. If we had a little piece of land, at least, it could have make a difference. Perhaps I could afford to miss a day now and then. But as thing stand, what to do? Child, make sure you pass and it will be worth it. I praying for you. Make sure of you future. OK? Not to cry. Not to cry, for me please, son. It hurting me heart to see you. But is for the best. Just do you best for me please, you hear, child. Not to cry. It hurting me heart.'

Willive needn't have worried about if Thunder would pass the exam. Passing and getting away from there was the reward to look forward to at the end of the eight months in that school. So Thunder passed. Always, afterwards, he said it was because he had no choice. The future existence he was concerned about then was more immediate than the one in his mother's mind. He has avoided every occasion to go through the doors of that school since, even though the headmaster has been dead some years.

School was one subject that made Ned Janvier lift his head to look at his son. And what he had to say was usually brief. 'Study you book, you know.'

Ned. It was as if he had locked himself inside of something called silence and thrown away the key. The silence he chose to live inside surrounded him with a gloom that had attracted Willive at first, when she saw him in the Soleil market. He stood up there outside of the rum shop with a drink in his hand, a tall, thin man with eyes lying down deep in his face. He was looking over towards the sea behind the fish market, and it was as if he wasn't even hearing the noise behind him, the pounding of dominoes, the men's voices raised high because they drinking and quarrelling. Willive looked at him and wondered what his story was, what made him look so sad and so silent. She circled the town and returned to find him still standing up there, leaning against the rum shop, a cigarette in his hand, this time smoking and looking at the sea. It was something in his face as he looked at the sea that made her decide, without hearing him speak a word, 'My spirit move with him.'

She was in the fish market, trying to shout above the heads of other people to make sure of a share in the big jacks that had come in, when she realised he was standing up near to her, looking at her and asking, 'How much you want?' She told him. He lift his voice and say, 'Macomere, give me two pound of jacks dey, nuh.'

Afterwards, he explained about the fish vendor. He knew her from time, he said. 'She from by me up there, by Paradise up there. We grow up in the same yard, not far from where

Workers' Row is now.' That day, he offered Willive a roti. They sat down together to eat, not saying much, but while they stayed silent, the spirit was talking between them. And is so the relationship start.

But the very things which had attracted Willive – the long, thin, stooped figure, the silence – after a while started to really irritate her. She was constantly telling him to 'shake yourself' and asking why he must look so much like the living dead. Ned greeted all of this with silence, so much so that after a while Willive relapsed into silence herself when he was around. 'Well,' she decide, 'when we say for better for worse, we hope is better, but if we get worse, what to do? Is not every time you buy a ticket you come out lucky. In fact, is once in a blue moon luck hit you. So what to do? And anyway,' she thinking, 'is not really worse.' She had never heard anybody call his name with other people and he wasn't a beating man. And there were so many of those about. Not that they would stay together if he was, but still.

In a way, she hadn't changed her mind about her spirit moving with his. Only that he kept his spirit locked up inside and hardly ever gave it a chance to peep out. It was as if, she thinking sometimes, it had more between the two of them than they ever manage to reach. More, in a way, than life let them share. Another thing, he never had money, although he worked all week, and that made Willive wonder sometimes if he had some secret responsibility stashed away somewhere. But one day she sat down and added up for herself how much he made in the hotel in town, how much he spent on transport, how much he had to spend on his uniform to keep himself looking good for guests, since the hotel only gave one free, and then she thought, 'Is not his fault, he don't have it, in truth, poor thing.'

She added up what she made in the Nutmeg Pool and realised that she didn't have it either, that was thanks to the shop that allowed them to take things on credit that they were able to eat. Thanks, too, to Mamag, God rest her soul, that they had a little spot behind the house where they could grow their own little fig and two cabbage and things like that. Mamag had made over the spot to them, with land paper and everything. It wasn't much, but it was a lot, and Willive's dream was to be able one day to see her son buy an acre or two. One day, one day, congotay.

'If you have at least one acre,' she said to Thunder, 'you could always turn you hand to something. Look at that, eh. Look what land confusion do to this family. Me? Because my mother was girl and not boy, she didn't have right to share in her own family piece and then it had so much confusion, like I tell you, in the land that should have been your grandfather own. And now look your granduncle Son-Son generation lose all through debt. So the family land gone right down. Look at us. We eating the bread that the devil knead because of family divided against itself. Get you own acre or even half acre as soon as you could, son. Listen to what I telling you.'

One day, while talking to Thunder about things like this, Willive was putting up some sticks for the tomatoes. Thunder and Ned sat on the hill looking at her, and Ned grumbled in his throat, as if to say, 'You right. You well right.' Willive just wished he would say it out, so Thunder would hear. She looked from one to the other, Ned now digging a little hole in the ground with his cutlass, Thunder heaping some dust around a cabbage patch, and hoped that somehow a message about life was getting through from Ned to Thunder.

Perhaps the message did get through to Ned that Willive wanted him to talk to his son, because all of a sudden one weekend, he started. Long afterwards, Thunder remembered that weekend in 1970, the year before he won a scholarship and went down to High School in Paz City, as the weekend his father spoke.

Ned came up that Friday evening on the bus called 'Nothing Venture, Nothing Win'. It was owned by a man who had ventured, to work in the Lago Oilfields in Aruba, and returned to set his winnings spinning laboriously on the streets of Paz. Willive and Thunder, sitting in the Nutmeg Pool above the road, watched Ned get off the bus in the crossroads by the Police Station.

'Look Daddy!' Thunder said, 'Daddy come up.'

'What strange?' his mother asked in a quiet voice. 'You didn't expect him to come up?'

Thunder went to the steps and looked down the road by the Police Station.

'You all right, Thunder?' Ned called.

Thunder grinned and looked back at his mother. It was the first time he could remember his father calling him by the familiar name of Thunder. When Ned called Thunder anything, it was William. Today, having called him Thunder, he shouted, 'Let's go up, nuh. You waiting for your mother?'

Thunder turned back to Willive. 'Mammy, I going up with Daddy, eh.'

'Yes. All right. I don't have long again. See you-all just now.'

Well, yes, thought Willive, *today, today, I see blood come out of stone.*

When Thunder had raced down the steps to meet his father and the two set off on the climb up the hill towards the

109

road down to The Dip, Willive muttered, 'Like Ned win a sweepstake. How he jolly so?'

The woman sitting down next to her shuffled the mace in the tray and gave a grunt that may have been laughter. Tongue and teeth doesn't laugh at good thing, nuh. So he have to win sweepstake to talk, *wi*?'

'Well, I don't know,' said Willive. 'I just hope is big, big money he win.'

Nigger-yard

Later, when Willive got home, Thunder was asking his father all kinds of questions about Paz City. And then he said, 'Daddy, tell me something about you. About how you grow up and so.'

Ned looked uncomfortable. 'Let your mother tell you,' he said. 'She good at that kind of thing; let her tell you. Nothing to tell, really. Is the same like you mother.'

Willive was unpacking the bag with his clothes. Ned glanced across at her. And Willive, not meeting his glance, started, 'Well, your father used to live . . .'

'You tell me the story, nuh, Daddy,' Thunder begged. 'Mammy tell me a lot already, about her father in the land and so. You tell me about you.'

Ned looked at Willive again. And Willive, looking past his head at the partition, advised. 'Tell him about growing up and so. Tell him where you used to live. Tell him what it feel like. Tell him the same kind of things you say your mother and your grandmother tell you about. Tell him about Dada.'

For a moment, Ned looked as if he would refuse, as if he would leave them and go and sit outside on the hill, as he usually did. Then he laughed and said, 'All-you this family! Is Mamag have all-you so. Well,' and he moved around on the chair, turning his body away from them, facing forward, clasped his hands, lowered his head to his clasped hands and sat biting on his left thumb. Lifted his head and looked outside, through the window, down the hill towards the mill. Then turned back and started to talk.

'Well, we used to live in a place, just ordinary, a place called Nigger-Yard.'

'You mean . . . ? They really called it . . . ? You used to live in Nigger-Yard in truth, Daddy? They called it that? Who called it so?' Thunder asked. His teacher had been telling them the day before about places which used to be called Nigger-Yard. They had all sniggered. And now . . .

'Well, nobody, really. Nobody call it Nigger-Yard. Was just the name, you know. Was so I know it. Everybody call it so.' Ned cleared his throat, turned his head away, shifted his body on the chair and laughed slightly. He looked at Willive, but she wasn't looking at him. 'Yes,' he said. 'Yes. Well, it was nothing, really. That was the name. Wasn't anything . . . wasn't anything political or anything like that, you understand? That was just the name. And . . .' he moved the chair, scraping it against the floor, turning it towards them.

This was not a comfortable subject. Everything that was happening these days in the country was political, and young people were talking so much about being black. As if, Willive said sometimes, they just discover. The place was a mess. She hoped Thunder wasn't thinking this political way. Anyway, he young still. Ned was continuing. 'And I remember, I remember . . .' And he turned again, looking out through the window and tapping his fingers against the table in the way that he did when he was thinking things out. 'I remember . . .

'A little board house, with three steps at the front, leading

114

up to the front door. A room and hall. Kitchen outside, bamboo. Bamboo kitchen under the mango tree. Was calivigny mango. Mango lung. Board house made of roundwood, covered with straw. Board house in the middle of the cane. At first, it was wattle and daub. Bamboo, you know, bamboo and cow dung. But not smelly. When it dry and prepare, not smelly at all. Just wattle and daub. But then they improve it. The estate improve it. And all the Nigger-Yard houses, about eight or ten of them, ten, yes. All get roundwood and straw. Things was better then. And a check curtain. A check curtain, I remember, in the door. Most doors. The door split in two, you know. Top and bottom. A check curtain showing in the top half. The half that usually stay open during the day. Nigger-Yard. That was Nigger-Yard.

'What I remember most,' Ned said, 'is what happen the time of the war. In the beginning was only a word that people use. War. We know it was serious, you know, but it was kind of exciting like. And then, well,' and he laughed, pulled at his chin with thumb and forefinger, cupped his left hand and rubbed it up and down along his right arm. 'Well, everybody wanted to play a part, you know. Seeing like how we was English then too and everybody was proud of England. So one day, I talk to the boss.'

'You were living in Nigger-Yard that time, and working where, Daddy?' Thunder asked.

'You working for a newspaper?' Willive asked. 'How you want to know thing exact, exact so?'

'In the estate house,' said Ned, laughing. 'Not in the field. Dada, my mother, work in the fields. But I used to work as the yard-boy. You know, seeing that everything all right around the yard, with the lawns and so. Cleaning the vehicles and the stables and so.'

115

'You did like it, Daddy?'

And Willive cut in, 'Is not like, is work. You do what you have to do. Is not like.'

'Is true, is not like. But, well, it wasn't bad. You have to do it, so you like it.' Ned said slowly. 'And it was better than the field work, you know. Field work was harder.'

'You like it, yes. For the time. And the yard work,' Willive said, not looking up from sorting the corn on the tray, 'the yard work had more prestige like.'

'Yes,' Ned agreed. 'Yes. Was more considered, you know.'

'So with the war, Daddy, what happen?'

And Ned was quiet again for a while, walking back in his mind to pick up the story. Then he continued, 'I talk to the boss. And he wasn't too encouraging at first. He just ask me, "You think you would like it?" Just that. You think you would like it? He tell me is a very hard life. He used to be in World War I, you see, and he say is a very hard life. He ask me if I sure. And he say, "All right." He will give me a letter if that is what I want to do. He didn't discourage me, you know. He was just . . . quiet like, quiet for a while, and then he say,' and Ned moved slightly on the chair, crossed his legs and lifted his eyebrows as he looked for Boss's tone: '"If you sure that's what you want to do, I'll give you a letter to take to the Major who doing the recruiting in Paz City. Friend of mine."' Ned chuckled, rubbed at the side of his nose with the forefinger of his right hand. 'He did know all this big people and them, you know. His people was here from long time, but is English extraction, so you know, is his friend. He know them.'

'They was in same bracket,' suggested Willive.

Ned agreed. 'Yes. Same kind of bracket. So the Boss, he give me a letter for the Major. Wait. Wasn't a major, nuh. Was a captain. Was a captain that was his friend. A Captain Johnson. So I went down. I went down to Paz City without telling Da nothing. All the time she think I up at the Great House. Captain Johnson was the enlisting officer. He send me to a Captain Jack Arthur to do a reading test. I remember well. I remember well. Ned chuckled again. Smiled a proud smile. When I finish reading, he say, "Good. That is the best we have had for the morning."' Ned smiled, looked from Thunder to Willive, looked away. Glanced across at Willive again. Rearranged his body on the chair. Said again, 'The best we have had for the morning. The best we have had for the morning.'

'What it was, Daddy? The reading test? You remember what they give you for the reading test?'

'Yes. I remember well. Just a line. "Many are called but few are chosen".' And he laughed. 'That was it. "Many are called but few are chosen".'

Ned looked into the distance through the window, remembering. Willive was shaking the tray of corn, blowing into it, letting the loose bits escape. And Ned continued his story:

'So after that, the enlisting officer give me the OK. And he give me a paper for the doctor, to do a medical test. And that was all right. So that day, I enlist with six others who pass the reading test.' He paused, thinking. Twisted his lips, rubbed his left thumb against the back of his right hand. 'That was June, he said. June 1945.

'After the test, I didn't have any place to stay in Paz City, so I walk back. Me and three other fellers from up that side. Walk all the way back up to Soleil. It didn't take too long. We leave town about four or five in the evening. Reach back to the Great House perhaps about nine or ten. Walk up. Pass through the Mon Riviere forest. By the lake. All of that wasn't like now.

Pure bush. And dark. And monkeys all through the trees. And mist. Wasn't like now. Was dark. And when I reach back, the Boss, well, he give me encouragement, you know. He say . . . he said . . . he was glad for me. Pleased, he say. But, he say, the army tough, you know, boy. The army not easy!

'Half past four the next morning, I left.' Ned stared at his son, through him, beyond him, as if willing Thunder to see the story with his eyes, so that he wouldn't have to walk back again. He was quiet a long time, almost as if he had forgotten them. When Ned looked at Thunder again, the boy's eyes were fixed on him, waiting. So Ned told his story and as he told it, he walked.

Walked on the green lawns with his bare feet that morning, instead of along the concrete path. Sometimes, looking at the grounds, he could hardly believe that he was the one who cut them and kept them looking so green and so smooth and so pretty. He walked down the hill, tried not to look behind. Walked across the flat, turned right on to the main road at the bottom, and right again, through the trace into Nigger-Yard. It was almost half past five. Two children, a girl and a boy, were walking with heads down, yawning, almost dragging milk-pan and bucket, going to the standpipe on the corner by the main road. They mumbled a greeting. 'All right,' said Ned. 'Morning.'

The bus for Paz City, he knew, would leave at a quarter to seven. Dada would be awake already. And yes. She was awake. As he went up to the steps, the door at the top was pushed open. Dada, tall, thin, sleep still creeping across her bony face, stood there with a box of matches in her hand. Before Ned could say a word, Dada put her hands to her head and started to bawl. Shouting, 'Oh, God! Oh, God! Trouble! Trouble, Papa God!'

She had been expecting something. She woke that morning with a heaviness. From a dream in which she was walking uphill. Which is good. But at the top when she came to this house, it was full of dead and dying dogs. A half-dead dog jumped at her, tore at her hand. The good thing was that she managed to shake it off and run out of the house, towards the top of another hill, to begin the climb down. Woke before she could begin the climb down. Which perhaps was also good. Now, in the middle of her bawling, the one thing, she said afterwards, that was making her feel a little bit good was that she had managed to shake the half-dead dog away. So what was it, then, this thing that had walked across her dream in the night and tried to tear her apart?

'Well, stop that, nuh,' Ned said, impatience grumbling in his voice. 'What happen to you?' he asked. 'What you making all this noise waking everybody up for?'

Then his sisters were at the door. Ione, getting rounder every day, pulling up the shoulder of the old dress she had slept with. 'What do?' they asked him. 'What do? What you doing here this time of the morning? Something do you? Boss fire you? What you do? What Dada bawling for?'

'I don't know,' he told them. 'Ask Da. Is she that bawling. She say she dream.'

He tried to push past them into the house. But they wouldn't move. Both of them just stood up there blocking his way and waiting for him to explain. Ned turned, walked down the steps.

'I just come down for some bread,' he said, looking up at them with exasperation. 'I come down for something to eat and I have to buy bread to bring back up.'

And Ione, arms akimbo on the steps above him, asked, 'Hard times hit Boss house? It don't have thing to eat there?'

119

But Dada, always anxious about food, calmed herself enough to say, 'Leave him. Come. Come and get something to eat. Sometimes in these people and them house, it not easy to put you hand on something. Come.'

Ned turned and walked up the steps. Bathsheba, looking as if she wanted to say something but was thinking better of it, stepped back from the doorway. Ione let him past, turned, followed him. Ned walked through the hall, lifting his feet over the bedclothes on the floor, opened the room door, stooped down and pulled out his grip.

'Dada,' Batsheba called, 'he packing his grip, yes.' But he wasn't packing his grip. Just getting something from it. They had told the new recruits not to come with anything. They would be given clothes.

Dada came in holding in her hand a branch with soursop leaves and a box of matches. She sat on the bed and watched him. Ned pulled a box from under the bed, rummaged through it, found his Royal Reader Book Five. A book that they told him used to be his father's. The last one he used in school. He rested the book on the bed. Looked at Dada. 'Dada,' he said, 'I going and eat something.'

In the hall, when the food was ready, they sat and watched him eat. Fry breadfruit. Breadfruit fried after last night's roasting on the fireside outside and saltfish that Dada prepared, washing it and then roasting it over the coalpot and mashing it up with a little coconut oil. And afterwards, the tea she prepared while he ate. Bush tea. Soursop leaf. Good cooling on this hot morning.

When he was finished, Ned went back into the room and pulled his black and white dress shoes out of the grip. They followed him. Walked in procession behind him. Then he stopped and turned. And, not looking at any of them, he said, 'Da, I going away. I going to Paz City today. I going and sign up for the war. I going in the army.'

Nigger-Yard woke to the sound of bawling. Ione and Bathsheba stood with Dada in the yard as Ned moved to the top of the hill to begin the walk down to the road. The early morning sky was a clear light blue, touched with fluffy white. Crickets were still singing the querulous tunes they had shouted all night. Cocks crowed in the distance. Any ordinary morning. Dada put her hands to her head, threw her head back and just stood there bawling. Dada put her hands to her belly, turned around in the yard, and her crying made the dogs begin to howl.

'Papa God! Oh, God! Papa God, look down! Is the dead dog, me Jesus. Me one and only boy-child in the world. Papa God! Woe-i! Woe-i! Is the dead dog, me Jesus!'

'Da, you waking everybody up, you know. Go inside, nuh.'

'Lord, Rock, you bad, *wi*.'

She always called him Rock. She had christened him Ned although his grandmother on his father's side wanted him called Batcha, after his father. Batcha because of his grandfather, Batcha, who had reached Paz in 1866 on a boat called the Countess Ripon. Batcha who had died of double pneumonia because of exposure, they said. She gave him Batcha as a second name. Her people in Eden wanted to call him Ned. She ended up having to give him three names to satisfy everybody. Ned Batcha Peter. Peter was hers. Peter the Rock. Ever since she was small she knew that her first boy-child would be Peter.

'Rock, you going in the army? Rock, how you bad so? Oh, God!'

121

'Da! Well, behave youself, nuh! he tried to get her to keep quiet.'

And Da bawled, 'Woe-i!'

All around the yard, the top parts of doors were coming open. Check curtains were pushed back and tied to one side. Miss Carmen stood tying her headtie and clearing her throat, Mr Maurice coughing and peering up at the sky to see what kind of day it was going to be. And then Cousin Dinah and Miss Mavis coming down the steps, drawling 'Morning all,' and walking over to Da. Saying, 'Take it easy, dousdous. Whatever it is, the Lord doesn't give us more than we can handle. What do? What happen?'

And Ned saying, 'Da, I have to get the bus just now, you know.'

And Cousin Dinah asking again, 'What do? What happen, Da? Where he goin?'

'Ask him! Ask him! Tell Cousin Dinah where you going! Woe-i! Woe-i!'

'Da,' he said, 'I going, you know.'

Miss Mavis put an arm around Ione. 'What happen, chile? What it is do all-you?'

'Rock going in the army,' Ione told her.

'Oh, merciful Jesus!' And Cousin Dinah swung round to face the yard, lifted her hands to the sky. '*Bonjay-y!* He going an fight war, all-you!'

Rock, feeling the tears coming, made a steupsing sound with his teeth and walked to the clearing to begin the climb down through the canes. The climb down the hill. Is the dead dog, me Jesus. Dada, Nigger-Yard following, walked down the hill behind him, bawling: 'Is the dead dog, me Jesus. Me one and only son in the world going and fight in the war.'

No breeze, that early morning. The trees didn't even move their leaves. Ned even remembered the scraggy dog that walked, nose sniffing in the dirt. He remembered that the dog sniffed at his feet, that he kicked at it. The dog moved away, slowly, and then stopped to look at him as he walked away.

Ned was crying when he climbed on to the early bus that came from Mon Repos, going through Soleil and on to Paz City for the mail. Crying and blinking his eyes and fumbling with his hands inside of the plastic bag in his hand so people wouldn't see his tears. Big man like him. Going and fight war and he crying.

Nigger-Yard was bawling as the bus started up and waited there for a while, engine running. Ned looked through the window, put his hand up and pushed at the tarpaulin which was drooping down over the window. Looked out from under his eyebrows to find Da. She was standing with her hands on her head and Cousin Dinah and Miss Mavis were holding her up. He couldn't look too long because he didn't know how to keep the tears from rushing down.

'Oh, God! The lady nice half-Indian son going and fight in the war! War! All-you, oy! Rock going and fight war!'

Da was crying, moaning, apparently. Ione and Bathsheba had their hands stretched up and waving in the air and they were bawling. The bus moved. Rock sort of half waved. A little wave. Brought his hand down from the tarpaulin accidental-like across his eyes. And under his nose. 'Is the dead dog, me Jesus.'

'So that was it,' Ned said now. 'That was it.' He put his hand down in his pocket as if he was looking for a handkerchief again. Laughed. Glanced at Willive. Cleared his throat. 'These things hard to remember, yes,' he said. And Willive, getting up to put the tray in the kitchen, agreed. 'They hard, yes.' Ned opened the window a little more. Looked outside. Continued. 'We had six months of recruitment training. Training in weaponry, drilling etc. Then the shooting range. Then afterwards, three months straight preparation for the Japanese. Then we left. Going on now. Going up.'

'Up?' Thunder asked him.

'To the war. We went to St Vincent. Join others, you know. Still training. Then St Lucia. But then, you see, after all that training, we were too late. Because the war end in 1945.'

'Thanks be Jesus,' Willive said.

'No,' Ned didn't agree. 'I was ready. We was well ready for them.'

'Ah, chut,' said Willive. 'You thank you stars, I sure. And if you didn't, which you insist, you should have.'

'No,' Ned still insisted. 'We were ready. We were well ready for them.'

'So what happen then? What happen then, Daddy?'

'Well, we didn't disband immediately. They kept us on, you know. Reserve forces, so we continue training. We didn't disband until forty-seven. July 1947.'

'Disband, what that mean, Daddy? Break up, like?'

'Yes, that is it. Break up, you know. Everybody going separate ways.'

'You were glad, though?' Thunder asked.

'Well, to tell the truth, I was disappointed. I felt ready to face the Japanese.'

'Ah, chut! *Manti tup*. Not true.' Willive is not convinced.

'True. True. And I was a good shot. I even get my first weekend off for excellent shooting on the range. The Japanese did frighten, you know. They see me coming.'

'Doubtless,' Willive said.

Ned laughed. 'All right. So don't believe. Well, later, when we come back to Paz, there was no work, really. And it was the time opportunities opening up in other places. People going to other countries, you know. And work opening up on the oilfield in Aruba. I remember I left with seventy others to go to Aruba on the *Island Star*. For those kind of travel that time, ex-servicemen had first priority. Because it had a lot of ex-servicemen, you know. People who join up and go to Egypt. Who go to RAF ground forces in England and so on. So come the end, first priority. But I didn't want to go at first, really. I didn't want to go away and work then. Some of me friends say I didn't have no ambition, but wasn't that. Wasn't lack of ambition at all. The first time I leave, you see, Dada take it so bad. And then by the time I come back she wasn't well, you know. And Bathsheba head was all for going to England when she could manage. And Ione, self, wasn't a kind of person you could depend on. And the Boss-man say he would give me a job as a driver. It wasn't paying much, but I was thinking of staying. Wasn't lack of ambition, nuh. Wasn't anything to do with ambition at all. Was Da. Was really Da. In the end, things was so bad I come and decide to go. But was me mother I was thinking about, really. Was Da.'

Thunder watched his mother's fingers moving now through the rice, choosing out the hard grains and pushing them to one side. He turned back and looked through the window behind him. He could see the dark outline of the silk-cotton tree in the distance. He moved to close the window and stood for a moment looking across The Dip, to where he had been told his great-uncle Son-Son was standing that time when Mamag cursed him off. He sat down again and watched the long outline of his father's jaw, turned away from him as Ned looked down towards the old sugar mill. In the distance, there was the faint sound of Carib's voice, shouting, 'Blood in the north, blood to come in the south, and the blue crying red in between.'

'Blood to come in the south,' Willive muttered. 'Sometimes you wonder what happening with Papa God world, yes. Blood to come in the south.'

Da

Sometimes, in the houses of his school friends in Paz City, Thunder saw paintings he recognised. An old woman, eyes distant and brooding, trapped in charcoal. An old woman, tall and thin, hands crossed above her head, eyes hunted, haunting. An old woman, right hand holding a pipe, face smothered in smoke. Sometimes, someone, a friend's mother or father, would find him staring and say, 'I see you like paintings. Lovely old woman, isn't she?' Thunder muttered some answer. But he kept thinking: *Is Da.*

'So elegant!' they said. 'Wolof, perhaps. Or could be Ashanti. Look at that height! So tall! So thin! Elegant and unspeaking.' *Da,* he thought, just sitting down there quiet on the wall.

Was Da. The complete opposite to Mamag, or even Gran Cassie, who was sort of quiet too, sometimes, Da sits silent in his memory. She stands with one hand on her waist, the other holding a pipe, making a sound in her throat, drinking smoke.

Da never seemed to have words. Never seemed to have a thing to say. Sometimes she tried. Looked at Thunder when he came close. Said '*Po-po-i*', with a smile and a half-stretched hand. But he would giggle and stand there watching her. And

Da would stretch her mouth out, long and offended. 'Go,' she would say. 'Get away.' Hissing it so his mother Willive wouldn't hear. She didn't mind so much if it was Ned. She would just say it out loud and not hiss if Ned was around, but when it was Willive, his mother, Da hissed at him, or looked sheepish, or was silent. Sometimes her neck tried to disappear down inside her body. When they were all together, she wouldn't sit at table. She would take up her plate, lower her head and say, 'I will eat mine in the kitchen.' And Thunder used to giggle. If Auntie Ione was around, she said, 'Lively up yourself, nuh, Mammy. How you doing cagoo so?' Willive would say, 'Is all right! Leave her if she want to go in the kitchen.' Ned steupsed and shook his head, looking frustrated. Willive would say, 'Well, she say she more comfortable there.' And the matter would be resolved as Da sidled off to the kitchen.

If their friends visited, Da disappeared into the room, or more likely behind the house or down the hill by the old sugar mill. If they were walking about the yard and surprised her sitting on a stone, or standing smoking a pipe, she tried to disappear inside herself. She shook a little girl's hand and said, 'Yes, miss. Pleased to meet you, miss.' She called her daughter-in-law, Willive, 'Miss Willive.' 'Yes, Miss Willive. All right, Miss Willive.'

Ned liked to invite her up, liked to have her staying with them, but Da never wanted to stay long. She always cried in the end, saying she wanted to go back to her two by four. Now that Ned had taken some time off and made a maroon to add on to the house in The Dip, it was a little bigger than Da's room and hall and she seemed more uncomfortable in it, not liking the change. Da, crying to go back to her own place.

'*Po-po-i?*' she called Thunder.

130

'Da, help me read,' he would beg.

'I would not in a cage be shut
Though it of gold should be
I love best in the w-o-o . . .

'Da, what is this word here?'

'Go,' she said, 'go!' gesturing with the hand not holding the pipe. 'Don't bother me. Go and ask you mother! Go!'

'Da!'

'Look, child, leave me alone. Go, I say!' hissing it at him. And her bottom lip drooped, trembling with anger. Thunder would cry as she pushed him away.

When Ned took Thunder there to visit, to Workers' Row, where Da lived, Da came outside in the yard to meet them. Sometimes they just stood in the yard for a while. Sometimes they went inside and sat on the chairs around the table. Da made lime juice with a lot of sugar. And smiled a lot. And looked at her hands a lot. She lived in a house up a hill. Room and a hall. Rock had had it painted. Had bought the chairs and the dining table. Had built up the kitchen. Most of the other houses around were a room and hall, unpainted.

'And that place,' Ned had explained to Thunder after he asked, 'that place was around where Nigger-Yard used to be. Just a little higher up. After the hurricane, you know, they had to build up again. A lot of mud come down in the old Nigger-Yard, so most people get new hurricane house a little lower down, but Nigger-Yard was just a little higher up. I never really talk about it before, you know. I didn't look at it as important. Is not the kind of thing you just go saying. And that is before. That was long-time.'

Da, Ned told Thunder, liked to quote from the priest and the church, 'Thou art Peter and upon this rock I will build my church.' She said it with pride, always, looking at him, smiling as if they shared a secret. 'And now,' Ned had said on the bus down to town with Thunder when they were going to the place in Paz City where he would be boarding, 'is you that is the rock.'

PAZ CITY

'Blood in the north, blood to come in the south, and the blue crying red in between.' Thunder, Calvin, his friend from Content who had also won a scholarship to the college in Paz City and Mark, their new friend from Paz City, stood at the top of Market Hill and watched Carib zigzag her way up.

Crocus bag slung across her back, Carib walked way over to her right, looked up and shouted, 'Blood in the north,' looked down and muttered to herself, zigzagged her way back across, and again, moving further up the hill each time. About three-quarters of the way up, she stopped in the middle of the hill and turned to face the sea below. She let the little crocus bag, tied and half-folded somewhere around her waist, fall behind her, lifted her hands up so that the folds of her white caftan fell around her. Except for the brown of the crocus bag behind her, and possibly the colour of her face and the fact that she was woman, she looked like Jesus looked in the pictures. 'Blood in the north,' she shouted, 'blood to come in the south, and people oh-h-h-h! Listen! The blue crying red in between. You can't see the red to come? The blue crying red in between.'

She turned when a bus horn honked behind her, and moving

to the side, continued her progress up the hill, repeating in conversational tones, 'The blue, I tell you. Crying red in between. Red. Red. Red in between.'

'That lady well mad, yes,' commented Mark. Thunder and Calvin exchanged a quick glance.

Thunder turned away, saying, 'Let's go up by the school and play some table tennis.' The others agreed and turned left up the hill with him, going up to the school.

For Thunder, there were lots of grey days in Paz City, the ones that the weather made grey and the ones that were filled with demonstrations about Black Power. Thunder joined these demonstrations sometimes, at first because his friends were going, and then because he started to link the Black Power idea with all that he knew about Da and Mamag and his grandfather. But sometimes, too, the demonstrations made him hear thunder roaring inside his head and he just went to the place where he was boarding and lay down in his room.

Sometimes he went down to the hotel to look for his father. This meant a five-mile walk down to the beach, since there was never enough money for bus fares. His scholarship barely covered boarding and enough for books and bus fares up on the weekends. And even when he went down to see his father, he wasn't comfortable letting Ned see his fear of thunder. At twelve, he would still go and stand close to his mother at the sound of thunder. With Ned, although Thunder felt better because his father was there, he didn't go close, but just closed his eyes and grit his teeth. He didn't see his father's eyes full of concern on his face. By the time he opened his eyes again, Ned was usually looking towards the sea, or had his head bent, concentrating on something else.

It was really during his third year in Paz City that Thunder began to take his studies seriously. Partly because Willive kept warning that she could see him heading for nothingness, which was a real sorrow when she considered how hard she had tried to keep him away from the nutmeg, and partly because he had needed the first two years to adjust to the pleasure of not having to study just to get away from the strap.

It was during that third year, too, that Ned talked more to him about his family.

One Saturday afternoon, at home in Content. Willive sat at the sewing machine and looked through the window. Down the hill, Ned sat in his favourite spot, on the big stone just above the new road that cutting through below the house and making all the trees disappear. When he was home, Ned would sit for hours and hours, staring at the old sugar mill that they could see clearly, now that the trees were cut down and the road built. An old crane, shamed by rust to silence, curved over the aged galvanise of the mill. Ned would sit there staring, and what he looking at, nobody know, because is not like in long-time days when the mill was full of noise and bustle and trucks dropping cane to grind and sugar boiling inside. The mill was quiet these days.

Thunder sat there with him today, and looking down at them Willive thought that it was a blessing, really, that the boy had gone to school in Paz City. Since then, the two had come to know each other better and these days they were actually talking. Ned talked more to her, too, as if he was suddenly coming alive. Thank you, Jesus, Willive whispered to herself. You work in mysterious ways in truth. Musbe Mamag up there helping you out.

Down the hill, from across the new road, the rattle of a bucket. Someone coughed, spat. Thunder and Ned looked across the road. One of the children from the house on the hill over on the other side was going to get water. No water in the pipe as usual. It probably went to those big tourist hotels in Paz City. Although, thought Ned, the hotels never get enough. Sometimes, he knew, they had to make their own arrangements.

'I don't understand,' he said now. 'I don't understand why with water all around us, we never have water in the pipe.' Thunder grunted, not understanding either, and not having any explanation to offer. 'They teach all-you that yet?' he asked Thunder.

Thunder shook his head, making a mental note to ask one of his teachers to explain.

'Morning, Mr Ned,' the little girl called, on her way up the road to the stand-pipe. 'Thunder.'

'OK,' Thunder muttered.

'Morning,' Ned answered, turning his head, looking at the child, moving his eyes back to the millhouse and the old crane curving over it.

The child walked slowly, the thumb of her right hand in her mouth, dragging her feet along the newly-paved road already beginning to sink and crack in the heat.

A droning sound overhead. The girl stopped and turned, her eyes scanning the blue sky. A boy, about nine, a year or so younger than the girl, ran up the road to meet her. His shirt was unbuttoned, the tail flying in the wind. The girl moved her eyes from the sky to his running form. 'Button you shirt, boy!' she shouted. 'You just wake up, you want to catch cold to give Mammy trouble? She going give you. Button up you shirt.'

Automatically, Thunder did up a button on his shirt. The boy stopped, put down his bucket, obeyed his sister, his eyes also scanning the sky. 'I can't see nothing,' he said, 'but must be American Airlines. The American Airlines plane.'

'No,' she corrected him, 'is British Airways they say does come on a Saturday now.'

Their eyes were still scanning the sky, but the sound was dying away. They turned and walked up road to the pipe.

'You hear my name, Thunder?' Ned said without preamble, as if he was continuing a conversation. 'You hear my full name? Ned Batcha Peter?'

'Yes?'

'Well, you know what the Peter is. I tell you that already, about your grandmother and the rock. You know what the others is?'

'No. You never tell me. What?'

'Well, one come from the nigger side and one from the coolie side.'

'African and Indian, Daddy.'

'Well, all right. Is so we say it, you know, so that not nothing. But all-you young people these days with you ideas. African and Indian, then. African, in truth, yes, the Ned part. It come from a Ned in slavery days that dead right in the market in Eden. They used to have a Sunday market, long ago, in slavery times. You know about slavery times? I suppose you do it in school?'

'Some of it. We doing some of that now.'

'Well, you know that the big-up white people and them take people from Africa and bring them here as slaves. Ned, now, was a Eden man. I never bring you over to Eden yet, but that was where he was living. I don't know what his African name was, before Ned. But he was a slave in Eden, you know, and they beat him and kill him in the market. Just like how

139

you mother talk about somebody call John Bull that they beat and kill in she family.'

'We learn in school how sometimes was the driver they used to get to beat people on the estate.'

'That's right. Was a driver they get to beat Ned. In those times there, driver was there to beat people, to make them work, and things like that. And is like they didn't have no choice about beating and even killing their own kind, because they working for somebody else. Is a hard thing to accept that it happen, but is like we working against weself from time. Is a hard thing to accept, but is true. Ned used to work in the corn, they say, planting, reaping, sorting and things like that. But they say he always used to take the corn afterwards when they put it in the storehouse, you know. So he was kind of rebellious, like. Rebellious because he work for nothing and then have to hide to get a little bit in what he self work for. The wickedness of the world.'

Thunder didn't say anything. He had picked up a stick and was digging it into the soft red dirt on the hill.

'They beat him merciful,' Ned continued. 'Beat him until the body and the spirit couldn't take no more, and he go off and meet his Maker. And when the story of Ned get report in those official place like government and court and so, nobody speak up for him and explain what was what.'

Ned paused and sat looking across at the mill. He glanced across at his son. 'I listening, you know, Daddy,' Thunder said. 'I listening.'

'In those times,' Ned went on, 'only the white people that was in charge of estate that had voice to talk. Them and their friends in high society. The doctor, he was white too, of course, white jefe doctor. He say how is fits Ned dead from. From fits.

Half-hour after they finish beat him, you know. He dead from fits. From apoplexy, he call the word. Because his neck did so short, they say, he get fits easy. You understand? They beat him merciful and they say he dead from fits because of the shortness of his neck. Fancy that, eh?'

'In the market in Eden, that was, Daddy?'

'In the market. The centre, you see. Anytime they have a big and important thing that they want people to know about, was the market. So you find a lot of thing happen right in the market. All those market all over the place. We watching them simple so, but it have enough blood that shed in them. Those market and those forts in this country, was always big centre for deciding things, with blood a lot of the time.

So you see? What I telling you is, Ned couldn't talk for himself those times. And nobody of our people, the black people, the African people who they call slaves like Ned and so, couldn't do a thing to help him. So now is the generations to come, like you and everybody who getting a education, have to write Ned name in the ground, have to say all the things that Ned couldn't say. Have to write thing down, since writing is the fashion these days. And, child, slave is not shame. Is not you that do something. By you, I mean the person who was slave. Who to shame is not them, but is who put them so. The white people and them and those of we own African people self, not all, mind you, but those who greedy for money and selling their own people. But mind you, child, that is not nothing strange. Thing so happen in all country from time. In all generations. Perhaps not always slavery self, but people pushing other people down. But the point is, is the white people to shame. I know we have a style, we does shame as if the white people and them so important, and we self, acting

141

as if is we have to shame. But I want you to understand. Is something my grandmother, Da mother in Eden, always used to tell me before she dead. We have nothing to shame of in that direction. She wasn't like Da at all, you know, my grandmother. She did more bold, like. Da grow up with her, you know. But wasn't she real mother. Da mother die when she was a baby. Was neighbour to the lady I come and know as grandmother. Nothing to shame of, she use to tell me, my grandmother. Nothing to shame of.'

Thunder looked up at the sky and saw the clouds beginning to gather behind the mountain. He moved his eyes away quickly, looked at his father's face.

'You know is why I think to tell you this now?' Ned asked. He didn't wait for an answer. 'Is because I see the big friends you bring with you when you come and see me down in the hotel sometimes. Now their father so is high people. Paz City high-browns and whites and so on. I not saying you musn't have this kind of friend, too, but I just never want you to forget us here. And by us I don't just mean me and you mother. I mean all of us people around here, you know, that know red mud. Those big people and them, their people have yacht and they living on beach and so. Move with them, because with you education you might even have you yacht youself one day, so you don't have to be in we class, if you see what I mean. But don't go and get like those big people. Make them know how you think, so you could bring them round to how you thinking. Don't go and think like them, you see what I mean? Don't forget us.'

'What you saying, Daddy? Calvin and Mark is me best friends, you know.'

'I know. You see the same thing, now? I shouldn't of talk.

142

You think I criticising you friends. Is not that. But is not only Calvin and Mark you come down there by me in the hotel with. So I know. Some of the people you moving with, their people and them own hotel for their self.' Ned looked anxiously at his son, not knowing how to go on, how to explain himself, thinking of Da, not knowing how to explain what he was thinking, hoping he hadn't put something between himself and Thunder now, by talking. 'I like when you come down there, you know,' he said, 'and whoever you bring, I don't mind.'

Thunder didn't answer. Sat looking across at the old mill and feeling very angry. He wasn't sure why.

After a while, Ned got up and said, 'I going up in the house, now.'

Thunder brought his eyes and his thoughts back to the hill. 'All right,' he said. Then he looked up at his father. 'I coming up just now.'

And, as Ned turned to go up the hill, 'I know what you saying, you know, Daddy. I understand. And I will still come down in the hotel by you, you know. I like to come down there. I just thinking, that's all. But I know what you saying.'

Ned smiled, relieved. 'All right,' he said. 'All right. I just wonder if I shouldn't of talk.'

'No. I glad you talk. I know what you saying.'

Ned made a sound in his throat and moved off up the hill. Thunder sat looking at the mill a while longer. Then he moved his eyes to the clouds behind the hill and stood up. He didn't want to be out here if thunder started.

And later on that night, Willive marvelled to see that Ned found the energy to go up the hill by where Mamag's house used to be, to break some corn in the garden she Willive had planted up there after Mamag's youngest daughter left for Trinidad and told her she could use that part of the land.

And when the moon came back out, Ned lit the coalpot outside, and they sat down on the hill roasting corn. And without any prompting Ned started to talk. Shaking the corn around in his hand and laughing and looking at Thunder. 'Thunder! Ship sail.'

And Thunder, looking grown-up and sceptical, keeping his eyes on his father, answered, 'Sail fast!' And Ned came back with, 'How many men on deck?'

Thunder stared hard at his father's fist as if his eyes could see the number of grains of corn through the knuckles. 'Seven!'

Ned shook his head, keeping his eyes on Thunder's face. Opened his hand. 'Give me seven,' he said, 'but is five.'

'You see, Mammy?' Thunder chuckled, looking at his mother. 'How you husband could cheat so? He drop the corn on the ground so he wouldn't have to give them up.'

'No,' said Ned, laughing. 'Not true, nuh.'

'Is true,' said Willive, 'I see you too.'

Ned laughed and gave in. But then said, 'I not playing again, man.'

'Hopeless,' said Thunder. 'You can't bear to lose. Hopeless.'

In the late evening, the sky was a clear light blue.

'It have a boat in the moon tonight,' Willive said, pointing. 'You don't see a boat, with a long thing like a mast pointing up?'

'Yes. Yes. I see it.'

'The boat that bring you great-grandfather. You ever tell Thunder about him?'

'Who? Ned, Daddy? The one they call Ned?'

'No,' he said. 'The other side. The Indian side. My great-grandfather, name Batcha. I did start to tell you, but I didn't get to that. Apparently . . . apparently, my great-grandfather come here on a boat name the *Countess of Ripon*. Was after slavery days, you know, that they come and bring these Indian people here to work. Was about 1866, my great-grandfather come, they tell me. And they put some of those that come on that boat to work on a estate somewhere up here in Mon Repos. And my great-grandfather, he die not long after reaching here. He die of double pneumonia, because of exposure, they say. My great-grandmother was pregnant with my grandfather when he dead. Her name was Moniah. And she dead, too, when my grand-father was young. She dead because a cut on her finger give her lockjaw. And a lot of people dead in those times, from bad treatment, you know. Some of them get all this disease that was around at the time. Thing like lockjaw . . . and well, they say that was really like tetanus, you know . . . and yaws and all kind of funny disease.'

'Yaws?'

'Yes. Was like a malnutrition disease, sores all over and so. And they say that a lot of people dead so, from yaws. It had another relative of mine they say that fall sick on the estate and they get a boat to bring he and others that was sick, down to Paz City.'

'A boat, Daddy?'

'Yes. In those times, there, people use to travel down to Paz City from places like Mon Repos and Soleil and so, by boat. They say it take four hours from Mon Repos to Paz City, if even self was only about twenty miles. And they put them on this boat with no nurse or doctor or anybody that know about sickness, no food, no water, even. And they say that is how a lot of people, including a relative of mine that they did call Luchnaw, dead. When he reach down, he was near to dead, and he dead in the hospital in town, there. Was Colony Hospital it was at the time. Colony Hospital.'

Willive turned her head to look down the hill by the old mill where a man said once he saw a spirit with a cutlass. Although Willive had said in answer to that, 'Ah, chut! Who spirit stupid enough to continue carrying cutlass after it well escape this life already? All who here looking up, spirit self looking down? If that spirit so dotish, that is nothing to fraid. Chut! Spirit with cutlass what?'

What the big yellow moon with the boat in it was shining its light on was Willive sitting down picking the corn off the cob one grain after another, the coal pot to one side with the fire going out, and the coals looking like it turning to ashes. And then Ned shook himself and said, 'Well, things changing.'

THE LAND

There were two things really worrying Willive by the time Thunder was finished school at age seventeen. Exams successfully behind him, he was still afraid of thunder. He didn't rush to hold her now, but she could see his shoulders contract and his jaw clench, especially when thunder crashed out of a clear blue sky. The second thing was the succession of women friends he seemed to be cultivating. 'Look,' she told him, 'I am not one of those mothers who say to people with girl children, 'hold you hen, me cock outside. I don't like the way you moving. If you want to be with a person, you with somebody, but this running around with everybody not good.'

Thunder frowned and moved away, saying nothing. When Willive spoke to Ned he laughed and said, 'The boy young. He will grow out of it.' He didn't seem to be growing out of it, and just over two years after he left school, when Willive heard that a young Paz City woman called Lydia who was awaiting her A-level results, was pregnant with Thunder's child, she made the sign of the cross.

'At least the little girl manage to have time do she exam,' she said.

Thunder, now a clerk for the tourist board in Paz City, told his mother the news and walked away, not waiting for her response to it. Lydia was already four months pregnant, he said, and he had just been told. A few months after giving her the news, he told her also about a scholarship to England, to study Accountancy. Willive was delighted, but she couldn't help saying quietly, 'You see when you young people don't have no responsibility? Lydia, now, she can't take scholarship to nowhere. She have to sit down and mind child.'

'Mammy,' he protested. 'Lydia didn't even tell me she pregnant, you know. And is not as if we did close or anything.'

'Close enough,' Willive said with indignation. 'You had to be close enough, for what happen to happen. And pray tell me what difference it would have make if she tell you?'

Thunder didn't answer. Couldn't say to his mother what he would have advised.

Willive said, 'Man lucky in truth. God didn't only give all-you gold spoon, he provide bib for if in case the spoon don't work too well, gold how it is. Anyway, me son. I glad for you. Make the best of you time in England. Is a joyful day.'

That year, 1979, was the year that Paz City exploded in Revolution. After the years of demonstrations, of confusion, the government was overthrown. That is it, people said. This is the blood that Carib been preaching about all the time.

Aside from the fact that there was little blood in the revolution and general support for the move, Carib continued to preach.

She stood up on the hill by the hospital, looked across at the hotel over the sea on the other side and moaned, 'It coming closer, Lord. It here. Blood to come in the south, and the blue crying red in between.' In the market square, Carib seemed

150

to be going hysterical. 'Blood!' she shouted. 'Blood! Oh, Jesus! The blue crying red in between.'

As the years passed, Carib preached with increasing fervour: 'Blood to come in the south.'

In the Attaseat mountain-land, the trees – bois canot and gliricida and immortelle – seemed confidently unaware of how radically the times were changing. They grew as they had before, stretching up and trying to catch each other's sunlight. Nutmeg spread its branches and made the mountain so cool and full of shade that sometimes it seemed like another country, unaware of how hot the sun made the lowland.

Willive went up to Attaseat when she heard that mountain lands were for sale. Not many people wanted land up there these days. Mountain land was not easy to take care of. And now that land lower down was not only for people high in colour and high in money, mountain land was generally ignored. Perhaps it was because of the family story that Willive ached to have that piece of land now up for sale, the piece that had once belonged to her father and to her uncle Cosmos. Cosmos who had left for Trinidad all those years ago, and, as far as anybody knew, had never returned or been heard of since his brother Ti-Moun's death.

Willive wrote to tell Thunder about the land. She knew he had no money saved up yet, but perhaps one day he would be willing to stand security for her, so that she could buy it. She would take in extra sewing, or work as much as she could picking up nutmeg on the land once she had it, to make it pay. Thunder didn't write back for a long time, but one day he rang. Phoned her up in the Pool, as he did whenever he remembered that he hadn't written. He couldn't speak for long on the telephone, but he spoke for long enough to say that he was thinking about the idea, but there was nothing he could say now. They could talk about it when he returned the following year. He couldn't wait to come home.

Willive went up to see the land often. Was not surprised that it wasn't being sold. Mountain land. One lot near to it went, but that one remained. Besides, people in the area knew she was hoping to get it and even if they had the money, nobody around would deliberately go after it.

Willive hoped Thunder would help when he could. From the few letters that he wrote, she was able to piece together the story of his life in London. He didn't like it.

Stopping to ask directions on the streets, he watched people clutch their bags or hurry away without answering. And he wasn't sure whether he was learning about big cities or about being black in London. 'Excuse me, sir. Could you tell me . . . ?'

Silence. And he would stand watching a tall figure hurrying away, head down, hands shoved into the pockets of a raincoat. And he would always be wondering whether that avoidance of him was because he was black. Or because he didn't belong. Were black people who were born in London less sensitive to this avoidance than he was? Had worked out better ways of dealing with it, perhaps, he decided, but no less sensitive. English, he felt, meant white and *all* black people seemed to occupy a curious stateless category. When people rushed away, though, might it not also be that they were in a big city and trust was a dangerous currency? Thunder's uncertainty about all these things came across to Willive in his short, hurried letters. In the phone calls he made to her at the Nutmeg Pool. 'You have shares in the telephone company over there?' she asked him gently once. 'Write me nuh, dear. This must be costing you a lot.'

Every day, he told her afterwards, was a grey day. Even in summer, he said. Sometimes he felt so low that he wanted to give up the course and go home.

'Well,' said Willive, 'that one you woulda have to drink jeyes to do.'

'I know, Mammy,' Thunder told her. 'Is only thinking of you and the licks you make me take in primary school that make me stay sometimes.'

'Praised be Jesus,' she said, 'at least some good come out of the licks. It knock some sense into you head.'

At every opportunity while he was away, Willive wrote to remind Thunder how glad he must be of this chance, how he must be sure to make use of all that England gave him that he couldn't get at home. Afterwards Thunder said that he did try; tried to drink in as much of the opportunity as possible, for education, for meeting with people, for what people referred to as the expansion of the mind that travel offered. But he found the days grey and depressing. No hint of blue pulled him from the bed in the morning; it wasn't often that the sun warmed a day. Most times, sunshine was cold. The clouds hung low and white and he found himself, walking, mostly contemplating his feet.

England drove him further inside himself, listening only to the thunder in his head, too depressed to write home, his head too full of noise to allow enough silence to participate much in what was going on around him. He walked with his shoulders hunched and tense, waiting for the sound of thunder. It seemed to him that thunder was always there, and his hands always jumping to hide his face.

He left the country the day after the course was finished, returning, with a deeper silence and a degree in Accountancy, to begin, as he said, to sell the blue. His job, as an accountant attached to the Ministry of Tourism, did nothing to lift his gloom. Still, it was great to wake most times to blue days. And these were revolutionary times. But he returned at a time when people were beginning to ask lots of questions about revolutionary rule, and when, whispers had it, there was confusion going on in inner leadership circles. And around Paz City, especially near to Unity Tunnel, Carib preached, with mournful intensity, about 'blood to come in the south'.

Thunder rented a place in Paz City, visited his daughter sometimes, brought her small gifts, stayed a short time in an awkward silence, and left just as awkwardly. He knew that Lydia took Nehanda often to Content to visit his parents, and was glad of that.

Home again, Thunder talked to his mother, or rather, Willive talked to her son, about the piece of land in Attaseat. He didn't think it was a good idea.

'Mountain land, Mammy,' he said, 'not easy to take care of.'

'What you know about easy to take care of?' Willive asked him. 'You never had to work land in you life.'

'OK. So I don't know nothing. What you asking me for?'

Willive swallowed her anger. 'All I telling you, is that both me and your father agree that we will work to pay for it; we just want you to stand a security for us, now that you back and you drawing accountant salary in the Ministry.'

Put like that, there was no argument. Perhaps. 'The only thing I worried about, Mammy, is you-all taking land quite up there. Because it mean when you finish work, and when Daddy come up weekend, you-all have to go all the way up there to see after the land.'

'We think about that,' Willive said, 'and we were thinking perhaps it would be a good idea to move the house up there, on the piece nearer the road.'

Thunder looked even more concerned. 'Mammy, up there far, you know. If anything happen to you-all up there, you have to go so far for doctor and everything.'

'Well, up there not as lonely as it used to be. It have a lot more houses around, and where we discuss putting the house is on a piece lower down, you know, right near to the road. We know time moving on, son, and things changing. But is where you happy, you know.'

Thunder had one more argument he wasn't sure how to bring up with his mother. The more he thought about it, the more he felt, yes, he should go into this with them and buy the three acres of land, jointly with them, as his mother wanted, or even securing the loan. He didn't see how he could *not* do it. The second option, perhaps. He would stand security for the loan. But he must let them know what some of his objections were.

Thunder chose a time when they were all seated at table, eating the fried fish that Ned had prepared, his big speciality, with the bread Willive had just finished baking. Ned was in his usual seat, where he could turn aside to look through the window, down the hill to the old mill. Willive was on his left, the seat nearest the kitchen and he, Thunder, sat with his back to the window which looked down on to the deeper part of The Dip.

'Mammy, Daddy, I will stand security for you-all for the loan and give you a little bit every month, so that you will be able to afford to pay for the land.'

'Yes, that good.' said Willive. 'But why not just come in with us, then, and we take the land together? Is you alone we have to think about, so when we gone, is for you anyway. And since you giving us the money to help, just come in with us.'

'Look, Mammy, forget this thing about what will happen after you dead. That is not something to worry about. And, erm, well, you know I in the Party since before I leave. I don't want to have to own any property. Er . . . I . . . you-all go ahead and get the land if you want.'

'We want!' announced Ned, pushing back his chair and standing up. 'You damn right we want!'

'What is this? Radical talk?'

'Is not radical talk,' shouted Ned. 'Is nothing to do with radical. Is just not sensible talk. So we, how all-you does say the word, we petty-bourgeois, right?'

'Daddy, who say anything about . . . ?'

'Petty who?' Willive asked.

'The thing is,' said Ned, walking from one end of the little room to the other, 'Mr Thunder and his friends figure that to be a real worker you musn't own property.'

'What nonsense I hearing?' asked Willive. 'Look, I believe in this talk about change. I know you all for that and I glad, but this is a load of nonsense. Where you ever hear you discouraging people from having a little something?'

'And what is two, three acres of land?' Ned wanted to know. People having eight, ten acres of land in this place and still not having nothing. By the time you pick up the two grain of nutmeg or cut the two bunch of banana and get next to nothing for it, what property you talking about?'

'All who in big job,' said Willive, 'getting their big pay and who have friend in high places so they have something to fall back on, could talk their stupidness if they want. But you, my son, with not a bean to you name and nothing but the

156

little education you have in you head, what stupidness you talking?'

'Look, Mammy, I didn't say . . .'

'You say enough,' Ned decided. 'I talk to you since you in school about letting friend experience go with you head. Other people life is not yours. Land! You whole family history tell you what land mean and instead of explaining to friend, you sit down there listening to what friend say. Since you in school,' Ned is shouting, 'I warning you about friend. I tell you you have to teach them, too, because they know book, they don't know you life. What they know about land? You self you don't know nothing, but you family live it. So you know! All over the place government talking this talk about unec . . . how they does say the word? You piece of land uneconomic or how they does say the thing. Well tell them it too late to change now. We grow up with uneconomic. And who not in it looking for it. We used to that. Is what we know. Is we salvation as we know it. Uneconomic, my foot.'

'Look,' said Willive, 'if this is a problem for you, Thunder, we will find some way to do it. Not to worry.'

'Mammy, I not saying is a problem for me. I will stand the loan.'

'Thanks,' said Ned. 'We waiting.' He slammed the door on the way out. Walked down the hill to sit in his spot opposite the old sugar mill.

Thunder stood up and turned to the window, looking down into The Dip. Willive sat at the table, looking as if she didn't quite understand what was happening.

It was some weeks later that Willive realised there was something unsettling in the atmosphere all over Paz. She kept remembering that when she took Thunder along to see Carib all those years ago, Carib had said it would all come right in the end. Walk him back over his story, and the rest is up to him. Willive kept asking herself how a person who grow up knowing what Thunder know could talk this foolishness about land. Not want to own two acre of land because it wrong or it don't make sense or how they say the thing?

One thing that made sense to the people of Mon Repos these days, were the noises they heard in the night. Not the kind of sense you could explain with words. The kind of sense that left you trembling and afraid and wishing you could sleep the exact same sleep again to try and change your dream.

People talked about noises coming from the old sugar mill near to The Dip during the night. As if the big copper vats that used to hold the cane juice in the old days were being tossed about by angry hands. As if people were walking on the rusty galvanise roof of the mill. Although, if you looked out in the night, there was nothing. The noises didn't stop, but there was nothing to be seen. It seemed as if the rusty crane was creaking and groaning its way to a start. People said they could even smell molasses, although no molasses had been made there for years.

A man talked about seeing a figure dart from behind one tree and run over to another, up on the estate behind Workers' Row, the old Nigger-Yard. Something like a shadow, but when he reached the spot there was nothing.

On her way home one night, a woman said, she had seen a little man in the road, not too far from the old mill. A very short man. It was dark and she couldn't see his face, but he walked past her all of a sudden like he had been walking behind her all the time. He was sort of moaning, and saying, 'You see Ranger cut me down and now I have no place to go? You see?

You hear? Poor me. Cut me down and now I have no place to go. Ah wa!' Then all of a sudden this man disappeared, and there was nothing. Her father's name was Ranger, and just a couple of days before he had cut down a tree in the land behind the mill. This, the woman was convinced, was the spirit of the tree, homeless and roaming. She hardly knew how she got home that night, she said.

And there was Carib too, walking from Attaseat to Leapers' Hill, from Leapers' Hill to Paz City and back up again, shouting and weeping openly in the street. 'Blood in the south, I say. Blood in the south, and the blue crying red in between.'

The days were clear and bright blue, but clouds like crazy in the sky at night. Everyone said it was a funny, funny time. In the night not only the spirits but the cats took over, screaming and caterwauling. There were the sounds of horses, too, racing in the night, and people spoke of balls of fire racing across the sky.

'Nation shall rise against nation,' Carib preached, in the road near to the Nutmeg Pool in Content. 'Nation shall divide against itself, and family against family. But bear up. It happen before. It always been happening. But don't let it happen again. All-you, oh-h-h! Don't let it happen again.'

Carib seemed to be completely possessed during this time. From the steps of the Nutmeg Pool, Willive made the sign of the cross as she watched her jump in the air and fall down, clutching her chest. Carib howled like a dog and cried like a cat. She kept repeating, 'Blood! Blood! Blood in the south!'

In the Police Station behind her, the police leaned over the bannister, watching and saying nothing. Some people thought perhaps the police should take her in, send her down to the mental asylum. 'She must be getting like the mother,' Content people who knew the story whispered. But Willive said, 'I don't believe she mad. Something in the air. I don't know what, but something in the air.'

From the steps of West India House, Carib shouted, 'Blood in the south, and the whole Caribbean in tears.' She stopped traffic in Unity Tunnel, preaching about blood and destruction.

In the market square, one Saturday, while people went about their business looking for peas and sorrel and ginger, Carib stood near to the war memorial and cried.

BLOOD IN THE SOUTH

T hroughout Paz and Eden, people talked about land. Young people like Thunder talking to their parents, politicians talking to each other, people with land arguing, people without land considering. In Paz City, government officials were concerned that the lots of land in the country were uneconomic, too small to be of any economic sense in the country's development plans, or even to provide any substantial income to the owners. Politicians on every side of the political spectrum seemed agreed on this. Even those out of government who, without talking much about it, were thinking of politics, agreed that these little lots of land were uneconomic. But the people with the uneconomic plots said, 'Them, they all right, yes. They could sit down there and talk through their ass. What they know bout land? If they never had land and get chance to have a acre, they would know about uneconomic. Them? They happy, *wi*. They could afford to talk through they bambam-hole.'

The government talked about land reform, about the need for a law which forbade the sale or purchase of land under five acres. From every part of Paz, letters were sent to the Government Land Commission.

A letter from Willive and Ned, written with Lydia's help and not shown to Thunder, read:

Dear Sir/Madam,

We write to say that we are very concerned about the fact that you are thinking of deciding not to sell land under five acres and not to allow people to buy land under five acres. In this country here, all country people, from a long time ago, own a little piece of land to help make two ends meet. If they don't own it, they trying to own it. A law like that will only be for rich people and for town people who accustom not having land and will leave poor people in the country in the lurch.

We hear that you are saying that the land is too small and that the country and the people cannot make a profit on it. That is poor people problem. The land is uneconomic for us as poor people because it little bit, but is what we could afford. From time, poor people have to pay more to live because they can't buy bulk. If you think a two acres here in Content village uneconomic, then you have some-body in another bigger country thinking the whole of Paz that all-you ruling uneconomic because it so small. Might be true, but is what we have. So you do away with me and my land and they do away with you. So soon, none of us will be there to tell the story. Perhaps that is the right thing, we can't say.

The land little bit in truth, but the answer can't be to say that it shouldn't be there. It seem to me that this way Paz will disappear very soon. Have a thought for poor people, because as a country, you poor too. All of us poor.

Yours sincerely

Ned Janvier and
Willive Janvier.

At first, the government and the various parties tried to encourage the younger people, people like Thunder who knew the situation from both sides, to talk to parents and explain the situation. This only served to cause confusion within families. Parents were upset that the very children who should know were trying to undermine them. It make you think, said Willive, that you shouldn't bother try and make them take in no little piece of education. Bury their nose in the nutmeg from the beginning and they will understand why land important to us, small as it is.

The Land Commission decided to try to lessen the tension around the country by holding a conference in the Market Square. Each village was asked to send a representative to talk about the issue. In the end, what the conference did was show how much feeling there was in the country around this issue. No village wanted to have just one representative in Paz City. Everybody wanted to be there. People travelled from Mon Repos and Soleil and Content and Workers' Row and every other corner of Paz. Some people even came over on the boat from the sister-island, Eden. The intended conference of village representatives became one big, open market forum for debate and discussion among various people. They stood in the market talking and shouting, and targetting the political leaders for abuse.

Willive pointed. 'Look, Ned. Look Thunder, yes. I sure that is Thunder I see over there standing up by the war memorial.'

'Stay here,' said Ned. 'I going and talk to him. I go bring him over. In fact self, come. Let's go, because it so easy to lose in this crowd.'

Thunder was standing near to the memorial, trying to

listen to what one of the government representatives was saying from the makeshift stage.

'But they not listening, Daddy,' he said when they caught up with him. 'Nobody listening to what the leaders trying to say, you know.'

'Well, we always listening,' Willive cut in. 'Now is time for us to talk.'

'But, Mammy . . .'

'Who side you on, by the way, Thunder?'

'All of us. Yours, Daddy own, mine, the government own.'

'How you go manage that, son? The government and them and us that have little piece of land, we saying different thing, you know.'

'Yes, but Mammy, I see the point because I know about land story . . .'

'Well, that is a relief! That is really a relief. And I say you forget. Ned, you hear? He know. You son know, *wi*.'

'What I saying is, eh, we have to find a way to let you-all own your little piece, but bring it together with a neighbour own and another neighbour own, so that when we selling things on the international market, it making sense . . .'

'That sound like boundary confusion to me,' said Ned.

'Yes!' Willive was emphatic. 'And you, Mr Thunder, you who know what land confusion do in you family, I don't see how you could be talking this nonsense about joining up . . .'

'Mammy, be practical.'

'Practical! Practical! Practical is word in book. I telling you about practical life we go through.'

The Janvier family had become the centre of one of the small, tight circles all around the market. One woman, a vendor who usually sold sive and thyme in the market, put in

166

her two pence worth. 'These children,' she said, 'I don't know where they come out with their fancy ideas. How you hear he talking there is just so me girl does go on with me. She that grow up in the yard there and know what boundary confusion do in we life. Now she talking to me about co-operative or how she say the word. Co-operative. You imagine that?'

'Well,' a man standing near to Ned cut in, 'is we that send them to school, eh. And is not all their ideas that bad . . .'

'How you mean is not all their ideas that bad? What you self saying?'

'Wait. Wait. What I saying is, a lot of these little piece of land, is true, they not up to much and if the young ones could find a way . . .'

'They up to much! They up to much for us when we ready for a market on a Saturday!'

'Well, yes. But that is just small potatoes.'

'We small! We well small! So is small potatoes we dealing with.'

'Look. This idea of federation and Caricom and all thing. That is part of it, you know. We have to come together to go forward!'

Voices clambered over each other for attention. So that the same voice seemed to be asking 'why' and saying 'is because' at the same time. The big circle broke up into smaller circles. And even smaller circles. Tempers rose. Vendors sold ice-cream and cakes and snow-ice. In the shops alongside the market, and in the booths inside the market, people sold rum and beers.

Some speeches were made, but people could hardly hear. For one thing, the overflow from the market square that Sunday was huge. People lined the streets way down to the sea, curving around to Unity Tunnel. It was not easy to hear. The voice of one speaker on the podium came through to people inside of the market. He talked about the cost of goods on the international market, high costs for small plots. The man on the podium fired tempers by declaring that people in Paz should realise that this was spinning top in mud, and stop this nana-pu-put in little plots.

Voices shouted back at him. 'Leave me let me make my nana-pu-put in my little piece of land. Is that I accustom to. Go where you don't have to make nana-pu-put on you thousand and one acre. If is nana-pu-put I making, leave me to do it.'

Afterwards, no one could say who threw the first stone. Who fired the first shot. No one. Except perhaps those that knew the first shots came from them. Soon the market square was a mass of people running and screaming. People rushed to buses, engines were revved up and horns were making a racket as drivers tried to find their way out of the market area. No vehicle was actually parked inside of the square, but there were a few around it. Those down by the seaside tried to make a quick escape before the crowds converged on them. People jumped into the sea to escape gun-shots and stone throwing. Some people took advantage of the confusion to smash store windows and remove goods.

When the major confusion subsided, Paz City was a mess of broken shop windows. Bodies of the wounded and the dead lay inside of the market square. Two of the government representatives and four members of the public lay dead. Several people were wounded. One or two of the walking wounded limped towards Hospital Hill, every so often looking behind, as if afraid the confusion might be following.

That night, Carib could not get into the market place

because it was guarded by the police. She walked up the hill to the hospital, sat on the wall by the mortuary, looking down at the sea. She was not shouting, not even talking loud, just muttering quietly to herself, as if the prophecy had turned on itself and was eating away at her insides.

AFTERWARDS

Months later, another monument appeared in the market square of Paz City. Standing next to the war memorial, it contained a plaque which proclaimed the gratitude of the residents of Paz to a Great Country which had intervened to grant monetary support for a land-reform programme which would bring Paz into the twenty-first century. A programme which, among other things, would gradually ensure that people were advanced enough money on reasonable terms to buy five-acre plots if they wished. And even if a lot of people still stuck to their one and two acres and didn't take up the offer because they had no way of beginning the payments, they were hopeful because the possibility was there.

Every Saturday now, Carib sat on the plaque and spoke conversationally. 'Still,' she said. 'Still we can't build a monument to weself. Blood in the north, blood in the south, and still we can't see is we that bleeding to build Paz. Still we can't see.'

Sometimes Carib sat on the monument and cried. Sometimes she stood up in white and looked up at the blue, shouting, 'Is the children, you know. They misguided sometimes, but is the young ones to stop the blue from crying red in between.'

And the market vendor said, 'Lower you noise, Carib, let me hear what me customers want. Two bunch of sive an thyme you say, Lady? Look, the carrots nice this week, yes. You don't want none?'

'Is the children, you know,' said Carib, conversationally. 'Is them to stop the blue from crying red in between.'

CARIB

S un hot. A blue day in Mon Repos. Just an ordinary day with the heat stroking your legs to wetness and running sticky hands across the back of your neck. Quiet. The children are in the school-house, and even from here you can hear a restless buzzing like mosquitoes singing. School soon done. The goat nuzzling at the grass as usual in the schoolyard and making you wonder, when it lift the head and look straight at you, chewing all the time, if is really true that goat mouth is bad mouth.

Carib will sit here in the graveyard until school over and the children gone home. Then later, when the sun gone down little bit, she will walk down east to Paz City.

She sits there on the gravestone and what fills her head is the sound of screaming in the hot silence. After all this time, after all these years, they are still screaming. They down there under the cliff where they jump from, she thinking and muttering, and people forget them. Gravestone knocking dog, yes, monument sprouting up like peas all over the place, but not one for them. Forgotten and drownded. The blue crying red in between. People come from far, far land, from all place miles away on the other side of the blue, and they asking, is here? Is here so? Where the long-ago people jump? Forgotten and consoled. Spare a thought, nuh. Watch them. You see them others how they chasing after the people? Lord! They jumping. Hear them! Hear them! Hear how they screaming. Forgotten and drownded. Forgotten. Lord! Oh, God! They gone. I can't watch. Is here so they jump? Yes. Just about here. They hiding in the bush. Hiding. Look them. Look them. Look them there.

Let me take a rest, you hear. Let me just take a little rest before I begin to walk down to Paz City. Sun hot. Let me rest. Hot. I don't want to fall asleep, nuh. But it hot.

Is dream or is wake? Want stone. Want gravestone. Memory. Want remembering. Bush choking. Want name. Is me. Is you. Want name. A gravestone. No name. No engraving. Stone. It fading. Monument. What it look like? *This plaque is dedicated to a Great Country* . . . They screaming. Oh, God! You hear them? You don't hear them screaming? Woy! It hot! Me head hurting. You don't hear how they screaming? Lord! Dreaming or awake?

Blood in the north. I have to shout when it spatter in me eye. Blood in the south, people! And look at the blue. Crying red in between! Oh, God! I sleeping. No, I awake, yes. What I dreaming? Plaque. Market. Turn around. Papa God, turn around! The four corners. Jesus! Make the sign of the cross. North, south, east and west. Lord, keep us safe. I must go. Sleeping and awake. Quiet and alive. Dead and screaming. Restless. Forgotten and consoled. And look me here. Sleeping.

I must go. Must walk. Make a circle round the land, you hear. Almost. Cut it in two with the walking. Walk through the heart. Heart hard there in the middle even though the breadfruit ripe and soft. Forgotten and drownded. Look at that, eh! They moaning. They crying. Here and over there. Everywhere. They happy over there, you know. But is over here they concern about. Below the rock. You not hearing them? By the old mill. All of them. From that time and from after. One voice and two voice. Three. By the hog plum tree. By the crossroads night time. You must does see them? And in the boundary, by the mortelle. And the blue. Just crying. Red in between. They screaming. All the time. You not hearing? North, south, east and west. The four corners. Make the sign of the cross. I must go. Schoolchildren coming out. Must go.

'Carib,' a little girl with her right thumb in her mouth muttering gentle gentle. 'You going down? You going to Paz City'?

But wait! Is what this now? What they trying? Stop. Look at the child, glance over her shoulder to see if others there waiting to pounce and to tease when you answer. Schoolchildren, you know. You can't take their time. One face now, then change quick, quick. Sudden, sudden. Before you look around. Who there? Who behind the bush? Nobody? No body. Is only them. Nobody else. Nobody but them. Forgotten and consoled.

'Yes, dear. I going to Paz City.'

And the child nod her head, twisting the plait and looking up at Carib. 'My mother working in Paz City, yes,' she says. 'She selling in a store. She does come up on the bus every evening. You know my mother?'

Carib shake her head, no. But for some reason the people under the hill screaming louder than before and Carib shake her head again, quick quick, yes. Yes, yes, yes. How I don't know? Yes. I just forget. I know your mother, yes. The child smile. Somebody know, doh.

'I like your dress, Carib. My mother say gold is for special occasion. It nice. Walk good, eh. Walk good, Carib.'

Yes. I will walk good. Is messenger, you know. Every little word that come to you strange and unexpected, no matter how little and how simple it look, is message. Don't look at it like nothing, nuh. Everything is one thing.

What story the sea know? Look at it, eh! And the mountain, what story it hiding? Walk back. Just look at life how it going! Watch the mortelle! When rain coming, mortelle bathing cocoa face with tears. And you see Crapaud? Four foot in the air now from saying wait a while. But not time for waiting again. It happen. Time come and pass. And was not only long time ago Crapaud listening to ground and saying wait a while, nuh. Is today. Today day self self. Standing up in the middle of the road in this modern day and thinking car light will stop if it just hold up the two front foot to say wait a while. And you see Crapaud as a result? Dead in the road. Four foot in the air. Wait a while? No more waiting, nuh. And hot as it is, things cool, you know. Things well cool.

Mortelle, it never die. When people having confusion over boundary in land, once one could remember where mortelle plant as a boundary, no need to shout. Confusion done. Mortelle root never die. Who know the place where the root is have the secret to finish the case. But still if you look at it one way, the story don't change. So perhaps is to wait a while. But keep out of the road. Keep out of the road. Crapaud, stay in the drain. Watch mortelle how it crying long-eye water on cocoa leaf.

Blood in the north, you know, blood in the south and the blue crying. It crying, you know. You hearing it? Red in between. But mortelle know the story from the root. Let's wait, eh. Time will come again and pass again. Wait for those that know the boundary mark.

But I walking still. Right through the heart down to Paz City. Through the heart. Forgotten and drownded. Not them alone, nuh. The blue crying red in between. You see this crocus bag over me shoulder? This one nearly empty. Light. But you ever see how they packing nutmeg in it? Full, full. Cocoa too, you know. To send away. To far country. Is here they jump? No. Up there. Behind there. But all over, you know. All over the land. They screaming. Forgotten and drownded. Drowned. Drown dead.

You walking with me? Come, come. Let me show you. You see this shop here? Time when thing come and turn ole mass, people from Great Country who come with plan they call land reform used to sit down inside there sometimes, and they talking. Talking. Word. Magnificent. Magnificent land. They think I don't hear, you know, but I hear them talking. The blue crying red. People didn't mind. Is a true word. They say thing come so we can't solve it weself so Great Country should come. Didn't mind. In between. And who mind, not saying. Watching and waiting. The way how thing come and pass hardly anybody know who was friend, who was enemy. Mother and father and sister and brother. Friend and friend. Enemy and enemy. Watching and waiting. Nobody know who is family, who is stranger. Only know red. In between. Who know the story? Family? Perhaps. Blood come, blood go, yes, and the blue still crying red. In between. Stranger. Holding your hand so nice and so soft when road get rough, you self you don't even know what is what, who is who. But blood in the north, remember, blood in the south.

They used to sit down in the shop behind there, just talking. Young boys, yes. Young, young boys from Great Country. And friendly, people say. Friendly. Friendly with who know where trap door situate inside their own house. Know the story. Even walk back if you find the way. But that is the problem. If you find the way. Walk back and know the story. Somebody children, them too. But dead body. Bodies. My head hurting. People on the other side screaming. You hear them? But not for themself, nuh. They all right. They going on. Is another beginning. Is who left behind. At least remember. To go on. Without shame. Forgotten and consoled. *Woy-o-yoy!* The blue. The blue. The blue crying red in between.

Mouth open, word jump out. Land little bit. But land big, you know. Big, big. Road long to walk. Well hard. Yesterday and today. Tomorrow.

Look at that now, eh. Look around. Weather changing. Just little while back, when we walking and talking, sun was so hot and burning. Now look at that. Is like the day getting dark. Just so, light turning to darkness. You never could tell with this September month, you see. Rain and thunder. And the blue crying red in spite of everything. In between. Still. Is who to stop the blue from crying? Is day, but it getting dark.

Jaloux, they call this place right here. Day getting dark, yes. Was right here, you know, people nice young children get shoot and get kill on this Jaloux stretch. Everybody children. And for what? One side and another. Land. Boundary. Confusion. Darkness. The wind. You hear the darkness? Cricket and all get bazoodee, singing in the drain like is night. But they right. Is night. Darkness. The wind. In between.

You ever listen to what cricket singing? Listen. I lift my foot put down from one place to another and the crickets, they singing the footstep. You hear them? You not hearing them? Is day but is night. How time come so, eh? Is day but is night. Listen. Listen. You hear how they singing?

Send me to tell you
Send me to tell you
Send me to tell you

Walking. Walking.
Watching. Looking.

Send me to tell you
Send me to tell you . . .

Lord have his mercy! My head hurting. You hearing them? You
not hearing them? Music in darkness. Music! In darkness.
Listen. Listen. Listen, nuh. You must could hear them. You
don't hear the drum and the shak-shak? Wait wait wait! Don't
talk yet. You don't hear the little peeny-weeny cricket keeping
time in the back? Listen. You hearing it? Crying red in between.

Ping. Ping.
Ping. Ping.
Crick-et. Crick-et.
Send me to tell you
Send me to tell you . . .

You hear them? Listen, listen, listen. Don't talk. They crying.
They crying. Hear the tears in their throat and the way how
they screaming? Is the long-ago people, you know. Jumping
and screaming. And crying just like children. Like cat in the
night. You not hearing them? *Wo-o-o-y!* Like lajabless. You
hearing them? Like is baccu somebody leave. *Wo-o-oy!* The land
full of noise. The river. Is the river, now. It far away, but
you hearing it? No. I not going up there. Not now. Not now.
I walking. Walking. From that house in the cocoa under the
church there, some nights you hearing the river all down here.

183

And people screaming. All in the river. Huh! They have story to tell. All-you, oh! The blue crying red in between. Still. Up to now. It dark. It dark. It well, well dark.

If people was washing in the river, this darkness must be take them well sudden. I hope they reach home. Praise God something will come, you hear, some time, to light up this darkness. People know. They know, you know. We know. Forgotten and consoled.

Look at that. Look, look, nuh. You see that? People lighting lamp and switching on light in their house, yes. Pix. Pix. Matches striking. Light going on. Is one, one people have lamp they control on their own these days, yes. One, one people. Is not lamp days that you could light up and put out for your self, you know. Is other people far away with switch, saying when is light, when is darkness. Putting on light. Taking out light. And their light always going. One lick. Pix. Leaving you in darkness. Hold on to your matches, you hear. In the north, blood. Blood in the south. And the blue still crying, you know. *Woy-o-yoy*! But it only looking like darkness. Stay awake, you hear. Don't go and sleep. Light just taking time to show. Is dark, but never mind. Is day.

This place here. You know it? Look how time come and pass, eh! After one time is another. Long ago, long, long ago, big shots, buying and selling. People get put off estate like was sack of coconut that too much in the way. How to forget that? You think stranger know that? You think Great Country care? But you know. Grow up with the colour of the mud on the hill. So what could make you forget? But sometimes who know the most does act like they know nothing at all. Head come and turn. But turn round again. Going be all right. Is just thunder inside. Will roll till the time come and pass.

Blue. 'Colour of forgetting' a woman call it one time, yes. Was the sea in Paz City she was watching. You hear the word? Forgetting. Not for who know. Walk back. And remember. Is red mud on the hill. Walk back. You never hear about John Bull? Colour of forgetting? The blue or the red? In between.

Is in the bush there, yes. In the bush up there Thunder go and stay after trouble take place in the market. Leave his mother house and walk up in the woods to listen. And listen. Sh-h-h! In the bush. Too much noise in the world. Thunder. Sometimes the children who should know most end up acting like they know nothing at all. But he will be all right, you know. He can't help it. Is his nation. It is written. Blue crying red. From there to here. England, they say, for education. And the bush. Walk good. He know the hill. Come back to walk back. Walk back.

Was yesterday. Is not today. Is tomorrow. And the crickets still making a racket in this night that is day. All the house and dem close up. Batten down. You see dem? You hearing the radio? Listen. Is hurricane warning. You listening? Shop window open to sell the last candle to light up the darkness. You want to sing? Let us sing. Let's sing, nuh.

> This little guiding light of mine
> I'm gonna let it shine
> This little guiding light of mine
> I'm gonna let it shine
> This little guiding light . . .

Ay Ay! Nigger-Yard they used to call it long time, you know. That place up there on the right hand side over the bridge. But it change up today. Was Nigger-Yard they used to call it.

185

Nigger-Yard people live round here. Yesterday was wattle and daub. What to do? Yesterday and today. You hear the blue? It still crying red, you know. Things changing? Wattle and daub. Big house. Things changing. But the blue still crying red, though. In between.

Storm. You hear about storm? Who there? Who there? Who behind the bush there? Oh, is you? You walking with me? Shame bush? Close up when you hit it. I know. I remember the story. She with you? Yes. I know you there, even when I don't see you, self. Storm? Well, when it come, it uprooting big, big house and putting them on the river to sail down to the sea. Big, big house, you know. And meantime, the little one standing steady and safe in the cocoa. Oh, is why you come? Little house in the cocoa. Little, and nowhere to go. But it have place, you know. Sometimes. I know, I know. People always thinking is them do thing but is who with them that they not even seeing. From before. Forgotten and consoled. I know. And you know sometimes is same little house that have to shelter the high-up ones who house river take?

Paradise. Paradise they call this place we passing through now. Pretty name. Word again, eh. Word. Magnificent. Pretty, pretty sky. Pretty sea. Pretty all round. Magnificent, is how they say the word.

But rain in the mountain. You hearing it? Paradise River. Even jookootoo Paradise River. You hear it? Growling from the rain in the mountain. You hear it? Well, it get jookootoo now. Was roaring once, though. Long time. But you hear how it grumbling? Something under the surface. Road dark. And you hear Crapaud? How it croaking? But we not waiting no while. Thing come and pass.

Soleil. This is the place. You know Soleil? Not a light. Watch the sky. Down there by the sea. Can't see. Not in darkness. Who there? I say, who there? Oh, is you? But what you crying for? Don't cry. Time coming. Consolation. Remembrance will reach. You used to live in Nigger-Yard up in the back there? Long, long time? You work on estate round here too? Oh, I see! But is all right. Remembrance coming. The blue. You can't see it. But you know sometimes right over there the sky does be bending down to suck on the sun red tongue when it sinking? Right over there. Blue sucking red. When it hot and it bright. You can't see it now. But the darkness will pass.

And listen to the wind, nuh. Listen to that wind! Ay-ay! You here too? All of all-you outside tonight? Everybody come? Welcome. Welcome. Forgotten and consoled. Welcome. Everybody outside. Inside. Look at that, all shop close, yes. No window open nowhere. All curtain close up tight and people praying inside. Nobody outside.

Pity my simplicity
Suffer me to come to thee.

I does still pray that sometimes, yes. Pray it and sing it. But then time come and pass, you see.

You hearing the wind? Just stay quiet and listen. Listen. Come on. Come on. Let us go.

You see this place? Golden Sand, they calling it. Golden Sand. It is written. Is the foolish man that will build a house on sand. But when sand is all you have, what happening then? Is not the foolish one that won't build no house at all? And what happening if sea come up and say sand belong to it? What happen then, eh? But don't worry. It may never happen. Is a word they say you always use, yes, my mother. Even after

187

it happen. But then perhaps you thinking that was only one happen. One. And is a lot of happen that amount to a something. And then time come and pass, and more thing happen. But if you use up all you worry now, what you will do when time really come to worry? I don't want to laugh, nuh. But sometimes you have to laugh. You have to laugh, you know. Stay there and don't laugh! Don't worry. Take night and make day. Don't worry. Is night, but is just a different kind of day when you get accustom to it. And anyway, is not long before another day. Not long. Not long. Not long at all.

Ay-ay! Who is this man walking in the road when all house batten down? And storm coming? Papa God! Is day or is night? Is dream or is real? Oh I forget. What I asking? Is real dream. Is man? Is not one of us? Oh, is one of me. Talking. Carib, you mad no ass walking the road in this darkness? Sh-h-h! Don't say nothing. And him outside too, you know. You see Ranger cut me down and now I have no place to stay? Huh! People from other world talking. Sh-h-h! He must be going to put in a animal that he forget outside.

This area where he living here, they cross the water, you know. The blue crying red in between. Boatload of people from India. You hear the screaming? Forgotten and consoled. You not hearing it? And you hear the crickets again? Listen. Time come and pass. The wind. Stay quiet. Sh-h-h-h! Just stay quiet for a while and listen. Umm? Listen.

Walk with me. Where you going? Oh! Some other somebody coming? Walk with me, walk with me. Time. You know time? Remember time? Well, it going. And coming. House come and build. They say with house build spirit have no place to get comfort in darkness. But it have place. I know it have place. Yes, I agree. House is not the only place. Is space that is place. Uh-huh. Tell them. Forgotten and consoled.

Look. Look up there. It dark, but you could still see. On that hill up there, that big house always quiet. Big house up there, yes. Over the sea. Grand, grand house. People coming back to retire. Coming back to die. Young people from long, long time they leave here, now turn old. Come back and still trying to forget what they never remember.

Hear the wind how it howling. Up there is the place call Après Toute. Far up. Far, far up. But I not going up. Not today. Another time. Is darkness in truth, yes. Look around. Not even one somebody in the rumshop. Not a candle. It getting late, too. People sleeping. Is not day any more. Is night and is darkness. No candle. Is September. Not November. But your eyes brighter than mine in darkness. Tell me, nuh . . . Where you? Where you? You gone? Where you? Where? Woy! Woy! Where . . . ? Sh-h-h! OK. I won't shout. I just didn't see you, that is all. I just didn't feel you, that is all. I didn't feel you, for a while. Stay with me, you know. Stay with me. Is dark but is day. Stay with me, eh. And everything going be all right. Stay with me. Let's walk. OK?

Perhaps I should turn left there, you think? Just in front there on the corner. Turn left and walk down through where they building all the new house for people that come from away? No. You want to go down in the market? Oh, is me you want to bring there? Why? OK. OK, then. I will walk the road right down. Want to walk up the hill and go under the prison, anyway. By the mad house. Sh-h-h-h! Say it low. Not to shout. By the mental asylum. Forgotten and consoled.

I want to go down there so when I reach the hill by the fort I could stop for a while. Want to turn back, too, just to look at the fort. You know? Up there in the darkness. I wonder if I will hear them tonight? Those footstep that not walking. I does hear them floating, you know. And the howling. And you know they say some footstep is people that can't even find their body. Is true? But how that could be true? Worrying about body, even on the other side? Oh, they want to put here to rest. To satisfy the mind of who there and who coming? So coming back to look for a toe. And a finger. But is OK still if they don't find it? Oh, it will help if we remember? Well, sprinkle holy water. We will sprinkle some rum. Some cane juice. Some remembrance. Some peace. Forgotten and consoled. Not to worry. Is not long before day.

I want to walk down the hill and look at the prison. Just to look.

Perd Temps, they call this place. Perd Temps. You see that bridge there? Remember it from long time? Ever know it? Once, they say, a man, walking home with drink in his eyes, see two black cats playing on the bridge in the middle of night. Jumping. Turning round. And prancing. Changing position. And scratching. Play turn to fight. Man watching. Cat voice start sounding like man voice. Man get frighten and raise foot to run. And pass out. Just so. Pass out cold, stretch out on the ground. Perhaps was the drink. Wake up next morning lying down on the roadside not far from the bridge. And see a dog, standing up like jefe on bridge. Big, black dog, yes. Growling. And licking. Who know if story start in the night and finish in day, or is what? So they say. Was dream but was real.

Sky getting darker. Is night. And is late. Where you, now? You disappear? Don't do me that, nuh. Oh, you here. You just trying to frighten me, you know. Making me walk alone. Don't disappear. Don't go. Is not long before time. I so want to reach.

No more blue in the sky, nuh. Not even a star anywhere. Is dark. And is night. It have a house on the hill up there. Jefe house from long-time. You know what they always saying? Spirits up there. As if that is a surprise. As if all-you not everywhere. But they don't know, you see. And fraid when they feel you. They don't even know is to fraid when they *can't* feel you. Close their heart. Thing getting ripe but heart still can't feel. You can't blame them, though. Is so time come. Time come and pass. But those spirit up there, people say it sound like they vex. A lot must be happen for them to vex. Considering. Forgotten and consoled. Listen. You hear anything? Is day but is dark. You hearing anything? Or is me to hear? You know? I don't know. They say knife and fork always clattering in that house on the hill. A party from long time? Estate house. House full of secret. And who know what is what? Not to tell me? Not yet? Another time. Every thing have it time. What is to know will know. Is to listen.

How to forget all the things that we never remember? Huh! Talk soft. Let me talk low, you hear. People sleeping. Is dark and is night. Sleeping. And dreaming. Talk soft. Police Station over there. Talk soft. Talk quiet. Talk soft. Sh-h-h! Disturbing people as usual. Me? Disturbing nobody.

> I'm going away
> In a sailing boat
> And if I don't come back
> Throw way the damn baby.
> Brown-skin girl. . .

Sh-h-h. Stop the singing. Quiet. Sh-h-h. And listen.
I know these children, yes. See them grow. How not to cry?

Lord! I reach the top. By the fort. By the . . . mental asylum. Right up there by the bush. I didn't say? But you know. I stand up there the night when people from Great Country guarding the gate. I remember his face. How to forget it? He never did want Great Country coming in to find no answer. Say land confusion is ours. Ours to mess up and to fix. His face like the thunder inside him. But sometimes is children that know most that act like they know nothing at all, yes. But it will be all right. Frighten and tie up like it was when man shoot man in the market. Over land. Again. In south as in north. And me under the truck. Watching and seeing. How to forget? Pow! Pow Pow! *Wo-o-oy*! Sh-h-h! Talk soft. Pow! Pow pow! *Wo-o-oy*! How to forget? Watching one another and in between, the darkness. Like night. How to forget? *Wo-o-oy*! Sh-h-h! But who know exactly what is what?

Over there, the prison. How to say more than that? Is the blue that talking. Moaning. Crying red. In between. The prison. How to say what people don't know? The prison. We know them. Know the mountain where they born and the river that flow down to the sea where they swim. They kill people in the market, they say. Over land. We know how they juke crayfish out from under river stone and the titiri they catch in basket in river mouth. The whale, the dolphin and the shark. And the thunder inside them. Same water. Story from long time. Lord have his mercy! The start of dream. And when dream turn to nightmare. In the market yesterday. In market today. Blood on my face yesterday. My father, my mother, my son and my daughter that is and is not. Same person. Today. Everything is one thing. The blue crying red in between. Long time. Seeing it still. Who come from far away and who inside. Who know? Forgotten and drown dead. Enough is enough.

Know the dream. Know the nightmare. Walk. You walking with me? Is you talking? Is me. The blue crying red in between. Still. You there? I hope you there, you know. Yes you there. Stay with me. Don't disappear, nuh. Stay with us. Is the children, yes. Is them to stop the blue from crying red in between.

All-you, oh! Listen. The blue still crying, yes. Red in between. But something coming. We listening. Consolation. Around and around in a circle. Red. Blue hungry. Is the children. Blood in the south. Stop the blue from crying red in between.

I could stay here in the crossroads, yes. Stay here by the roundabout and sleep. *Mwen las.* Will rest for a while. My body hurting like is somebody else own that they lend me. It not fitting. Who know? Time must be near. You with me. Still, look at it. Is day but is night.

Hurricane coming any time. Never know what to expect. Road hot but it cold. Look down there. Paz City. Pretty, eh? Even in darkness. Watch how the light from those houses looking over the water. Darkness. Covering the town. Covering the sea. But still it well pretty. Like Mon Repos. Like Content in the cocoa. And, you know, is not only darkness to think about now. Is the storm that coming. The blue swallow up. Swallow up by the grey. But still, all round the harbour, house full up of light.

Let's walk, you hear. Let us go. Town people don't sleep? Swipsing past in their car. They don't hear the hurricane warning? Swipsing past in their car. Those buses come round the corner like raymabuddy. Not seeing. Not hearing. They say God watch over those who don't know how to look after themself. Lord have his mercy. The blue crying red. And time come and pass.

British West Indian Airways coming in to the airport. The Miami flight, I hear them say. Miami. Paz. Taking out people. Bringing in people. Going to forget. Coming to forget. The blue crying red, I tell you. But in between. Quiet like, now. Coming, and going. Is night, but is not long before day. Is blue. Is red. Is only the young ones to stop the blue from crying red in between.

And is right here I will sit down for the while. Right here. Let me take this white sheet out of the crocus bag, spread it out and rest. Is here you want me to come, not so? Well I reach. Spread out the sheet over plaque and Great Country monument. Oh all right. I see it now. Cover it over and lie down nearby here in the market square under the blue. Not in red, nuh. Not in red at all. In gold. Dark or no dark, hurricane or no hurricane, I will lie down here until daylight come back. Daylight. And celebration. Lie down and rest to get back the strength. Stay with me, eh. I know. I know. I know you have no place going. Forgotten and consoled. Remembrance coming. Is blue. Is red. And is the young ones, yes, to stop the blue from crying red in between. Can't see the sun. But it coming. Is night, but is not long before day.

THUNDER

The Mon Repos beach. Once, a school friend of Thunder's had disappeared there. Water peaceful and greyish blue right up to the beach and then, a few feet out, rumbling water, tugging and pulling with the rocks. A shark ate the boy, people said, but Thunder could never get rid of the idea that the rocks had eaten him. Reached out and pulled him when no one was looking. At the funeral, the boy's uncle kept saying, 'Is like these children think we dotish and them self have sense. Not to go, not to go, not to go, you telling them. But no. Not to blame the dead, nuh, but these children they just never listen.'

Thunder walked down from the lake where he had sat watching the water, walked out of the track, turned left and walked all the way on a blue day. Decided to go home. To visit his parents. Almost there, he decided instead to turn right and go down to the beach. Walked in to the beach and found Ned sitting there.

Thunder stopped, wanted to creep away, but something in the way his father sat on the tangled roots of the trees, his shoulders drooping forward, his eyes on the water, made Thunder walk up to him.

'Daddy?'

Ned looked up, made a sound half of greeting, half of surprise, sat back, cleared his throat, coughed, bent down to pick up his red and white packet of cigarettes. Local, as usual. The match-flame flickered, went out.

Thunder sat down. Ned smoked, watching the sea. Put his head back and looked up at the sky. Watched the sea again.

Thunder tried to remember when was the last time he had said more to his father than 'Morning, Daddy.' He thought of 'Evening, Daddy.' And counted the letters. Same amount.

They had never found a way back from the quarrel about the land, especially since the government had crashed around that confusion. Around the blood in the market. People believed that those in government who had different views about this land business had used the market to settle scores. That brother had ordered the killing of brother to ensure support for a land policy that said no buying and selling of five acres and less. 'Blood in the south,' as Carib had shouted, and the whole Caribbean was in tears over this killing and tragedy.

Ned and Willive had gone ahead with the Attaseat land, because Thunder had guaranteed the loan for them, before giving up his job and going off into the hills. 'What a blessing,' Willive said the last time he visited her, 'that we buy this piece of land when we could. The payments not easy, but we will make it. We bound to make it. At least you have something to fall back on.' Still thinking of him.

Two white tourists, a man and a woman, perhaps in their late sixties, walked along the beach. Ned cleared his throat and after a while said, 'This is we wealth, you know. The beach. The sea. The sun, even. Is the wealth that Paz have.'

Thunder picked up a twig from the beach and started stripping it.

Ned smoked. Half laughed. 'You don't agree?' he asked. Thunder was surprised. His father asked as if he wanted to know.

'Yes. Perhaps. In a way.' Thunder didn't want to talk about it.

Ned shifted, threw the cigarette butt into the sand, watched it glow, put his shoe on it, took out another cigarette. 'You know,' he said, 'your grandmother couldn't read.'

Thunder turned to look at him. He almost said, 'Yes, I know,' but then he stayed silent. Ned coughed some short, sharp, dry coughs. 'You smoking too much, Daddy,' Thunder thought it but didn't say it.

'You know,' said Ned, 'is why she never used to talk much. Especially with people that educated, you know. She used to feel, kind of stupid, like. Not that she was stupid, you understand me, but is, well, is just a feeling, like.'

Thunder turned back to watch the sea, how the water crashed over the reefs. 'I wish I had known Da better,' he said. 'I wish I had talked to her more.'

'Ah, well,' said Ned, drawing on his cigarette. He coughed that dry cough again.

Thunder looked at him. 'You smoking too much, you know, Daddy.'

'I does say that sometimes, you know. But I smoking for so long, now. Is about thirty something years. Is too late to do anything about that. I too accustom to it.'

'But I don't like how that cough sounding.'

'Don't worry, man. But you right, you know. Sometimes I does feel a kind of tightness in the chest here so.'

'You never check with the doctor?'

'All those doctor and them not really listening to people like me so.'

Thunder turned again to watch the water. 'I will go with you one day, if you want. Next week?'

'Well, OK. All right, then. Let me know when you ready.' And then after a while, he said, 'Your mother always telling me I should check the doctor with this cough, you know. She will be glad to know that I decide to go.'

Thunder looked at his father and said, 'Is all right, Daddy. It going be all right.' And for the first time in years, put out a hand and touched his father. Saw the tears come to Ned's eyes.

'What about Nehanda, Daddy? You still see her sometimes?'

'The grandmother bring her up to see us every now and then, now that Lydia gone in Jamaica to study, but they don't come often, you know. I suppose, it not really exciting for Nehanda. And she getting big, you know.'

'Yes, I know. I went to see her last week.' Thunder was quiet for a while again, watching the sea, and then he said. 'Is a shame, I know, that I have nothing to give her. But that will change. Just yesterday, I was thinking of something that Mammy tell me.'

Thunder didn't tell his father everything about that conversation with Willive. He didn't say that his mother had said, 'You is me son, but honest to goodness it sicken me to see how all-you man could ignore you children, not to talk about youself. Is true you never had nothing, but if you did figure you had responsibility, you would know you have to find it some way. She, the mother, she didn't have no choice. Is why all-you could talk so much about life, because you don't know not one damn thing about it. Sounding jefe and somebody else doing all the work!'

But Thunder told his father other things. How he sat down

by the plaque in the market that day of the darkness. Thinking of his daughter. And of him, Ned, and Willive.

Thunder told his father what his mother had said about a day she went down to the airport with Nehanda. 'I bring her down there to see the planes. And afterwards we went by the market to look at the monument they build to the Great Country that suppose to be solving we problem. The one the president unveil. And you know what she tell me when we stand up there reading that it is in honour of the Great Country and what it do for Paz? She ask me, Gran, it go be something, eh, if John Bull name was there, and Ned name was there and if we had a monument for Carib people and things like that? And I thinking, *I proud of you, child*. Mamag would well proud. Ned name will write one day. John Bull name will write for sure, because the generations didn't expire. I thinking, too, that with little ones thinking like that, the dream Carib have will come to pass. Everything is one thing, like Mamag would say. And there is nothing new under the sun.'

'Yes,' Ned said. 'Yes. You mother tell me the story. Thunder, you remember what I tell you once, about knowing the colour of the mud on the hill? The way you grow up, you know it. Just remember that, and you can't lose road.'

'I been thinking about that,' Thunder said. 'And Daddy, I don't know what you think about these things, Daddy. But is only yesterday I suddenly thinking. Me? I up there by the lake worrying about the past, but Nehanda, she in front. I don't know if you know what I saying, but the way how I feel is Nehanda generation, yes, that will write the names that we ignore all this time. Is Nehanda generation.'

And they sat there, Ned thinking of Willive calling, 'Ned! Come, nuh. Come and tell Nehanda bout you people.' And glad that even though he hadn't been in the mood then, he did talk afterwards. Thunder thinking of Carib shouting, 'Is the children to stop the blue from crying red in between.'

And as they sat, each wrapped in his own silence, out of a clear sky on this blue day, thunder crashed. It was some seconds before Thunder realised that he hadn't flinched. Ned realised it too. He looked across at his son, laughed, put an arm around his shoulder. 'So you is big man now?' he asked. 'You don't fraid thunder again?'

And Thunder tried to still the shaking in his voice as he answered, 'Yes. Me is big man now. I hope Mamag seeing. Me is big man now.' And he was thinking, 'I have to go and tell me mother.' When the thunder sounded again, the two men stood up and turned away from the sea. They walked towards the road. It was getting dark, but their feet would show them the way.

KICK-EM-GINNY
REMEMBERING

Every week, the boat moves twice from Paz to Eden and back. These days, with no volcano in the sea, the boat moves easily. A sign of the times, people say. Long ago was sail boat. Rocking more on the sea. A rougher water with blue the colour of danger and freedom. Nowadays is engine boats. Smoother. Rough round December. But not like before. Smoother.

Sometimes an old body might tense with the habit. But by and by everyone forgets where the spot is. Sometimes they pass right over, and a young body, with the taunting voice of a spirit she cannot control, would ask, that place in the water where they say the volcano does kick up, the place they call Kick-em-Ginny, where is it exactly? All-you sure it exist? The older heads smile, exchange glances. You better leave Kick-em-Ginny alone. You want to know? They shake their heads, as much as to say, these young people tempting fate for true. Tongue and teeth just don't laugh at good thing.

But no one talks much about it after a time. The older heads return to dust. And come again forgetting. And by-and-by Kick-em-Ginny disappears. People bury it and forget it, they think. For ten years, they have tried, too, to forget events that brought death and confusion to the market square in Paz City.

But now Carib is talking again about blood. About the killing and destruction that fulfilled her prophecy.

Sometimes people even stand up in the boats with hands on their hips, right over Kick-em-Ginny's heart, and say things like, this Kick-em-Ginny they talk about, it dead for true?

They say in some places there are snakes that look like a log of wood. If you go your way easy they leave you alone, but if you sit on their backs to rest they swallow you while you sleep. You have to be careful, people say, not to sit on the snake's back. Because afterwards, people would be watching and seeing the belly moving and not know what it is inside.

The sea turns over. The boat rocks only a little. People move one foot slightly away from the other for better balance.

A woman, bracing her body against the side of the boat, looks out into the midday sun. 'I remember one morning early, eh,' she said, 'going back to Eden from this selfsame Paz there, the boat lift up so, is like it settle it bam-bam on the point.' The woman gets up to cock out her bam-bam and lean over the sides. She is laughing. Tongue and teeth, as usual. Never laugh at good thing. The boat moves with her. 'It heave to one side,' she says, 'it heave to the other side, and I tell you, eh, was all man jack insides over the sides.' Arms reach out to steady the woman. She sinks laughing to her seat.

Today, the man they call Skipper rests his hand lightly on the ropes, looks at the water. 'All-you laughing? Take care you don't tempt the spirit in the water!'

'Ah, chut,' they laugh, 'Kick-em-Ginny dead, man, Skipper. That is backwardness. Superstition. Is alright, Skipper. Don't worry up youself. The spirit dead. You know, is a volcano they say that under there, you know. A volcano in the place where two currents meet that does make the water bubble up and kick up it backside against the boat bottom.'

'Volcano, spirit, same thing,' Skipper grumbles. 'Same thing. Volcano, huh?' His eyes watch the water.

'Is two current that was fighting in the centre there, Skipper, and one win out. Kick-em-Ginny dead.'

'Oh, so one win out, eh? Just so? After Kick-em-Ginny form it fashion there for how much years? Alright, if you think one win out.'

'Skipper, you too downhearted, man. The water cool. Kick-em-Ginny dead, I tell you!'

'All right. One win out.'

There is wood all around. Some even brace themselves against the wooden sides of the ship as they laugh.

The sea is blue peace, the colour of forgetting. No one thinks to knock wood.

Some of the people on the boat today, you can tell by their white skin and the way they squinge up their eyes against the sun, are tourists who have been having a fun weekend in Eden. They look around, all around, as if they want to be sure to see everything. They watch the sea. They look at the sky as if they want to swallow it and keep it inside. They say things about the blue. They say words like gorgeous and magnificent. They dress in shorts.

This Saturday morning, on *Huddersfield*, there are people going to catch the market. A woman is going down to Paz City to sell black wine. Everybody knows Eden's black wine is best. You have to know who you're buying from, of course. On the boat today, too, there are people who have been visiting relatives in Eden. There are two Trinidadians who are really from Eden if you trace it back far enough, and no further.

There is a man from Jamaica who is explaining to the woman sitting next to him that he had heard that people from Eden used their haitches somewhat like Jamaicans and he wanted to listen for himself and trace the story in the sounds. And a woman looks at him and says, 'Papa met! Talk you talk, me friend. All-you don't hear? The story in the sounds! *Amway bonjay*!' There are two students from Martinique who talk without stop. They speak English in a way that turns heads. 'You don't hear how they talking pretty?' the same woman says to no one in particular. 'Talking pretty, pretty, and black like me, yes!' The people around her shift in their seats and look under their eyebrows at the young people. On the boat too, there are children leaning over and singing to the water:

Day's done
Gone the sun
From the sea
From the hills
From the sky
All is well
Safely rest
God is nigh!

The seaspray leaps up at them, silver blue and shining.

There is a baby who sleeps, wakes and cries. While the child sleeps, the mother turns her head and stares down into the blue. Her eyes devour the sea. Her tongue flicks out every now and then to taste the salt on her lips. Near to her sits a woman in a faded, once sea-blue dress and a straw hat. Carib. She, too, watches the sea. An old man sleeps, sitting straight up. Now and then, his head bobs to one side.

The baby begins to wail. The woman-mother stands. The sea's belly growls. The woman with the baby walks. Pats. Croons. Sings.

DoDo Petit Popo
Mama gone in Mon Repos
Buy cake and sugar-plum
Give baby some . . .

Holds the wailing baby in its red and white patterned dress high above her head. She laughs up at the child, trying to change screams to chuckles. The child screams.

The sea is quiet. Blue but almost green. So blue you can't look down and see anything below its surface. Nothing but the blue-green and the sun glinting golden silver back into your eyes. The boat moves so smoothly it is standing still.

Skipper talks about his son in Huddersfield. When they go they never want to come back again, except to die. Although the little money does come in handy, you know. But still. Came to buy his boat and go back again to England. Young. So dangerous he thought launching and blessing a boat was old-fashioned. 'Bless it my foot,' he said. 'I have no money to splash on thing so.' Look at that, eh! A boy that grow up right where most of the boats building. What a way people change sometimes when they travel! Fact is, sometimes they stay right here and get the stupid ideas in their head. Still, they bless the boat for him. The whole family put a little to it. Most of it come from the selfsame money he send. These young people they know everything. And you could see Skipper touching wood, doing it as if by accident. And watching the water.

'Brace youself,' a woman's voice says quietly. Some heads come up, looking for the voice, watching the sea, listening.

'What happen?'

'Something happening?'

People sit up. The baby cries. The woman walks, patting, holding high, crooning. The old man is asleep.

Carib is watching the sea. 'Kick-em-Ginny!' she shouts. A boy giggles, his hand over his mouth. He is standing in the middle of one of his father's stories. The baby stops wailing to watch the laughing boy. The woman-mother's eyes move from boy to baby. She turns swiftly to rock unsteady and watch the sea. The boat lurches. The old man is awake, bracing himself with phantom terror against the boat, holding on to the sides and vomiting into the water.

Huddersfield is resting her bam-bam on the point of a mountain of water. The boat heaves to one side. The woman moves, staggers, fumbles towards a seat at the side. People are holding on to anything and anybody, bracing themselves, vomiting over the sides.

Carib is holding on to the sides of the boat, rocking with it and staring down into the sea. The man standing next to Carib touches her and asks, 'OK, sister?' And that seems to trigger off something that had been waiting for release.

Carib puts her hands to her head and starts to howl. A mound of water kicks at the boat-bottom, gently. And subsides. The boat bucks a little. Jumps again. Settles down. People begin to sink back into their seats, to lie down across the deck, moaning.

Carib stands, elbows close to her sides, hands halfway up, now wailing a sound that stays in her throat and stops only to start again.

The old man doesn't seem to recognise the faces around him. There is a trail of vomit on his lips. He wipes it away with the back of his hand. He grins. His lips quiver. 'That was a bad one, yes, Miss Mae,' he says, to no one. 'A bad one.' Miss Mae probably says some quiet thing, because the old man laughs. He explains that Miss Mae say is not so bad, really. That it's twenty years to the day since his wife, Miss Mae, went to meet her Maker.

The Caribbean sea is forget-me-not blue as *Huddersfield* chugs its way towards Paz City. White birds circle the rocks.

The sound from Carib rises and falls. Her eyes are now on the fort above the harbour. She points. 'Red,' she says. 'Red. You see it? The fort dripping red. Both sides of the wall, the two faces. You see it? Red. Dripping red. All over the country. The forts and the market and dem. Always dripping red.' Carib stands in the middle of the boat, turning around, hands to her head. 'Red,' she says, 'red. Red all over the fort. The fort like the market.' People prop themselves up on their elbows to watch the fort. Turn around to stare. Carib turns away. Around, hands to her head, bawling.

'Is OK,' someone says, seeing the uncertainty on the faces of some of the white tourists. 'Is a lady like that, you know. Ten years ago, when the troubles happen and people kill each other in the market square in Paz City, she prophesy it. Is so she is. Don't mind her. Is so she is.'

This doesn't seem to really make the tourists feel better. They move uneasily, and look from Carib to the sea for reassurance.

Tears and snot mingle on Carib's face as she walks, bawling, up and down the boat. Around boxes. Stumbling. Sitting down. Getting up. Around bodies. 'Oh, God! Is red. Is black. Is blue. Oh, God!' She holds on to the sides and looks towards

211

the bare brown face of the rock below the hospital. Below the fort. She turns around, tears streaming down her face. Is blue,' she says. 'But is red. Is blue. Is red. The good thing is, is more blue than red. But is to remember and to find a way to wipe out the red that there already.' She turns and stumbles her way to the sides. 'You see it?' she asks, pointing. 'You see it? The red. The red.'

People keep looking at the rock, back at her. 'Is like the colour the baby wearing,' she says. 'You don't see it? It bleeding. The rock bleeding.'

'The rock?' they ask. 'Not the fort? The rock? What happening? Something else happening again?'

'The rock. The rock and the fort. You don't see it? It happen already. It happen already. It not happening again. It happen already. You don't see? But we still don't know nothing yet. Blood come in the north, blood reach in the south, but we still not building a stone for we self. The spirits still vex, yes. Red. Red. The fort is we defence. The market and the rock have to get clean again. Red. Blood in the north, blood in the south, and is the children to stop the blue from crying red in between. The blue and the brown. The fort and the sky. The rock and the sea. Is the children, they saying, to stop the blue from crying red in between. But it not happening again, you know. It happen already. But is the children to know and to stop it.'

People are mumbling. 'Is the first time I hear her say that about the children, you know. You hear?' An old woman puts her hand down into her bosom, pulls out a rosary, makes the sign of the cross, kisses the rosary. A man bows his head and makes the sign of the cross, too. People move their eyes from Carib's face to the face of the rock, and from there up to the fort.

'Is so the time come,' someone says. 'Is the amount of evil that about. Is a lot, a lot of blood that shed in this Paz here over the years, you know. Not only today. From before slavery times to today.'

'The blue still taking,' Carib says in a quiet voice. 'The blue still waiting. The blue still taking. Until we remember. But it happen already. It happening all the time. The blue still waiting.'

The woman with the baby cries, 'Oh God Oh God Oh God! All-you help me with the baby!'

A man puts his head down and seems to be trying to clear the baby's nose, in a panic, trying to blow air into the child's mouth. People crowd around. One woman says, 'Back-back. Give the child air. Move let me see. I know about first aid. Move let me see.'

Someone says, 'It look like it choke on the vomit. Nothing to do. The child look like it done dead already, yes.'

'The boat is full of the woman-mother's bawling.

People look like they don't know what to say. Hands are up, half-cupped around mouths, eyes going wider and wider, people afraid to move. The old woman begins a prayer. 'Hail Mary, full of grace, the Lord is with thee . . .'

Other voices join hers, '. . . the fruit of thy womb, Jesus.'

Some people look slightly shamefaced as they mutter, as if they feel they should, but are not sure what they are really saying.

Carib stands looking at the rock, muttering, 'Red. Red. The blue still vex and crying red in between. But is all right, you know. Is all right as long as we see and we know and we remember. Is young blood. Is the young people to stop the blue from crying red in between. And it going be all right.'

213

Huddersfield, green, gold and red stripes circling her body, chugs into the harbour of Paz City. The weather has changed without warning. Grey-black clouds race across the sky to make way for the blue, or perhaps to challenge the blue. The sea is grey-green. White birds circle the red rock.

Also of interest from Virago

ROTTEN POMERACK
By Merle Collins

'*Rotten Pomerack* is the witty, passionate, long-memoried verse
testament of a singularly challenging, incorruptible and resonant
Grenadian story-teller' – *Michael Horovitz*

.

At the heart of this fiercely haunting volume of poems is an
ardent spirit of storytelling. Voices whisper or shout or quietly
call attention to some particular experience, whether personal
or political – the longing for 'home' wherever it may be and the
balm of forgetting.

.

RATTLEBONE
By Maxine Clair

'I love Maxine Clair's writing. She is a writer who should be read right now or folks will be missing out on something special' – *Terry Mcmillan*

In Rattlebone, a black community north of Kansas City, the smell of manure and bacon from Armour's Packing House is everywhere; Shady Maurice's roadhouse plays the latest jazz, the best eggs are sold by the Red Quanders and gospel rules at the Strangers Rest Baptist Church. Encompassing moods ranging from the richly comic, through the painful and poignant to real tragedy, this is a vivid, teeming, jewel of a novel.

WHOLE OF A MORNING SKY
By Grace Nichols

'She has the discipline of a poet; there are no wasted words or excessive descriptions, but a sure sense of what is sufficient . . . Nichols has wit, acidity, tenderness, any number of gifts at her disposal' – *Jeanette Winterson*

Along with the sweep of political upheavals – strikes, riots, and racial clashes – daily life in the Walcotts' Charlestown neighbourhood and beyond gathers its own intensity. Tension peaks one terrible night when the Ramsammy's rum shop is threatened with burning. In this her first adult novel, Grace Nichols richly and imaginatively evokes a world that was part of her own Guyanese childhood.

Books by post

Virago Books are available through mail order or from your local bookshop. Other books which might be of interest include:—

☐ Rattlebone	Maxine Clair	£9.99
☐ Rotten Pomerack	Merle Collins	£8.99
☐ The Ivory Swing	Janette Turner Hospital	£5.99
☐ Their Eyes Were Watching God	Zora Neale Hurston	£6.99
☐ Whole of a Morning Sky	Grace Nichols	£6.99
☐ Free Love	Ali Smith	£7.99

Please send Cheque/Eurocheque/Postal Order (sterling only), Access, Visa or Mastercard:

☐☐☐☐☐☐☐☐☐☐☐☐☐☐☐☐

Expiry Date: _____   *Signature:* _____

Please allow 75 pence per book for post and packing in U.K. Overseas customers please allow £1.00 per copy for post and packing.

All orders to:
Virago Press, Book Service by Post, P.O. Box 29, Douglas, Isle of Man, IM99 1BQ.   Tel: 01624 675137.   Fax: 01624 670923.

Name: _____

Address: _____

_____

Please allow 20 days for delivery.
Please tick box if you would like to receive a free stock list ☐
Please tick box if you do not wish to receive any additional information ☐

Prices and availability subject to change without notice.